BEACON STREET GIRLS

This book belongs to:

VERITAS AMICITIA GAUDIUM
truth friendship fun!

™

BEACON STREET GIRLS

Green Algae and Bubble Gum Wars

BY
ANNIE BRYANT

mix
ALADDIN MIX
NEW YORK LONDON TORONTO SYDNEY

This book is a work of fiction. Any references to historical events, real people, or real locales are used fictitiously. Other names, characters, places, and incidents are the product of the author's imagination, and any resemblance to actual events or locales or persons, living or dead, is entirely coincidental.

ALADDIN M!X

Simon & Schuster Children's Publishing Division

1230 Avenue of the Americas, New York, NY 10020

Designed by Dana Barsky

The text of this book was set in Palatino Linotype.

Manufactured in the United States of America

First Aladdin M!X edition October 2008

6 8 10 9 7 5

Library of Congress Control Number 2008931774

ISBN-13: 978-1-4169-6429-2

ISBN-10: 1-4169-6429-0

ISBN 978-1-4391-5962-0 (eBook)

0613 MTN

Who's Who

BSG

Katani Summers
a.k.a. Kgirl . . . Katani has a strong fashion sense and business savvy. She is stylish, loyal & cool.

Avery Madden
Avery is passionate about all sports and animal rights. She is energetic, optimistic & outspoken.

Charlotte Ramsey
A self-acknowledged "klutz" and an aspiring writer, Charlotte is all too familiar with being the new kid in town. She is intelligent, worldly & curious.

Isabel Martinez
Her ambition is to be an artist. She was the last to join the Beacon Street Girls. She is artistic, sensitive & kind.

Maeve Kaplan-Taylor
Maeve wants to be a movie star. Bubbly and upbeat, she wears her heart on her sleeve. She is entertaining, friendly & fun.

Ms. Razzberry Pink
The stylishly pink proprietor of the "Think Pink" boutique is chic, gracious & charming.

Marty
The adopted best dog friend of the Beacon Street Girls is feisty, cuddly & suave.

Happy Lucky Thingy and alter ego Mad Nasty Thingy
Marty's favorite chew toy, it is known to reveal its alter ego when shaken too roughly. He is most often happy.

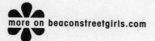

more on beaconstreetgirls.com

The publishers wish to thank everyone at Sally Ride Science for their invaluable contributions to the development of this book. Special thanks to Sallie Chisholm, Professor of Environmental Affairs, Massachusetts Institute of Technology, for reviewing the science on algae.

Part One
Green Algae

1

Science Shmience

It was a gorgeous, sunny day, but Maeve Kaplan-Taylor was not a happy camper. There was nothing quite as upsetting as watching her four best friends happily turn down Beacon Street on their way to their favorite hangout, Montoya's Bakery, without her. Katani, in her shiny silver-colored parka, was strutting ahead confidently. She was telling Charlotte and Isabel all about a fabulous sale going on at her favorite vintage store. Avery was jogging along behind the other three, happily dribbling a blue and yellow soccer ball. But Maeve, sadly, was left standing alone. *Now I know how that cheese must have felt in the song about the Farmer in the Dell. Poor little cheese!* Maeve thought to herself, dramatically touching her heart.

"Hey, Maeve, last chance—we really want you to come!" Avery hollered back, stopping her soccer ball under her sneaker. She beckoned for Maeve to join the group. "Think about it—a mug full of Montoya's chocolate deliciousness . . . ?"

"Oh, I really, really *do* want to go! But I just can't—it's my tutoring day. Have a mug for me, okay?"

"Okay!" Avery shouted. And with that she punted her soccer ball up the street and took off in a wild chase behind it.

Maeve felt like there were lead blocks attached to her feet as she trudged back to her family's apartment on Harvard Street. After all, this had been a bad, horrible day right from the start. It all began when Maeve overslept for the second time that week and had to run to school without breakfast or major hair repair. A triple tragedy.

Then worst of all, Ms. Rodriguez had given the class a pop quiz in English. Maeve hated pop quizzes more than anything . . . even more than practicing free throws in basketball. Studying for a regular test was bad enough, but to be *ambushed* with a test . . . right when she was *starving* . . . that was just too unfair! And . . . lunch, of course, was none other than the dreaded tuna fish mac and cheese—maybe the worst thing ever invented. A cup of hot chocolate and some quality time with the BSG probably would have been the one thing that could've cheered her up.

The tiny silver lining on Maeve's ginormous black rain cloud was her ultra-cute math tutor, Matt. *Matt, Matt, Matt.* Maeve thought he looked like Caleb Tucker, the adorable actor from *Maplewood,* one of her absolute fave TV shows. Plus Matt was a student at Boston College. Compared to the immature boys in her class like Henry Yurt and Billy Trentini, Matt the Adorable was a dream. In Maeve's personal opinion, all tutors should have to be adorable by law. *Oh! Light bulb moment,* Maeve thought excitedly. Maybe Matt the Adorable could even make her *want* to learn science like Charlotte and Katani—they were both crazy about math and science.

When she arrived home, she was relieved to see that Matt hadn't arrived yet. *Phew.* Now she had a chance to have a snack and freshen up a little. As soon as she opened the kitchen door, a heavenly smell wafted her way. *Cookies — chocolate chip cookies.* From the plastic wrapper on the counter she saw that it was the kind from a big block of pre-made dough. Maeve's mother worked and didn't have too much time to make cookies from scratch, but Maeve didn't care one bit. Cookie dough was cookie dough. Period, final. Next to the plastic wrapper she saw a note in her mother's handwriting: "Hi, Maeve — I'm on a conference call in my bedroom — cookies will be done at 3:15 — work hard with Matt! XOXO Love, Mom."

"Hey, Maeve! Think fast!"

Maeve didn't have time to think at all, because something hard — very hard — suddenly smacked her in the chest. "Ouch!" she cried, watching a plastic ball roll away. *That really hurt,* she thought angrily. Maeve knew just who was responsible: with fiery blue eyes, she charged toward the sound of muffled laughter behind the china cabinet. Sure enough, there was her little brother, Sam, curled up on the floor, obviously pretending to be some kind of ninja Army dude — his favorite pastime other than torturing his older sister.

"What is *your* problem?" Maeve said, sounding every bit as annoyed as she felt.

"Huh? What'd I do?" Sam blinked innocently.

"Don't play dumb with me, Sam. You threw that ball at me for no reason. *Hard!* And guess what? It really hurt!"

Sam's smile disappeared when he saw that his sister wasn't joking around. Sam liked to tease Maeve — okay, Sam *loved* to tease Maeve — but he never meant to hurt her. "I'm sorry," Sam mumbled. "I was just joking around. I thought you would laugh."

Maeve shook her head. How her brother ever thought that whacking her with a hard plastic ball would be funny was completely beyond her. "Oh, yeah? You know what makes people laugh?" Maeve asked.

Sam shrugged. "Um . . . what?"

Maeve mischievously raised an eyebrow. "You really wanna know?"

Sam nodded.

"Usually, this works every time." Maeve wiggled her fingers and went in for the kill, tickling her brother until Sam shrieked with laughter.

"I need rescue!" Sam yelled.

Suddenly, a male voice spoke from behind the pair of giggling kids. "Is this a bad time, Maeve?"

Startled, Maeve looked up and brushed her red ringlets out of her face. *Oops!* Just her luck! Matt the Adorable had arrived. Usually, Maeve strived to act like the glamorous future movie star that she knew in her heart she was. Why did Matt have to catch her playing with her little brother?

Sam jumped up like a Mexican jumping bean, while Maeve slowly peeled herself off the linoleum kitchen floor. "Hey, Matt, wanna see my new Astro fighter plane?" Sam asked.

"Psst. Out of here, Sam! Matt's here to help me, okay?" Maeve whispered fiercely. She glided over to the oven, used the heavy mitts to slide out the tray, and flashed her best camera-ready smile. "Would you care for a pastry, Matt?" she asked, as she transferred the cookies to a rack. "Pastry" sounded way more sophisticated than "cookie."

"Yeah, cool! Thanks, Maeve." He eagerly took two and gobbled them down. Maeve looked at him and thought dreamily, *This is just what it would be like if we were married. He'd get home from work. I would have a warm snack all ready and waiting. And I'd be wearing a little dress with short puffy sleeves and a red and white checkered apron, and my hair would be pulled back in a ponytail with a big red bow . . .* Maeve's daydreams were snapshots captured from all the old movies she watched on Saturdays at the movie theater her dad ran, which, lucky for her, was right below her apartment.

"Hey, Earth to Maeve, are you ready to get cracking on your science homework?" Matt asked, shattering her delightful fantasy.

"Science, shmience," Maeve groaned. "How about, let's not and say we did?"

"How about, your Mom would fire me?"

Maeve's eyes widened and she shook her head, feeling her curls brush her face. "Oh, no! I would never let *that* happen." She sighed, reluctantly slung her pink backpack onto the kitchen table, and pulled out her pink science binder. Maeve reasoned that if you had to do school stuff, you might as well surround yourself in pink. She once saw an interior design show that explained how the color pink put people in an optimistic frame of mind.

"I have bad news, Matt. I mean—really, really, extraordinarily, super-duperously . . . um . . ."

Matt raised his eyebrows. "Bad?"

"Yeah." She pulled out a sheet of paper and held it against her chest for a moment. She was sure that showing it to Matt would result in the end of the world.

"Okay, let's see it, Maeve. Is it another C?"

Maeve blushed, a little embarrassed that *that* was Matt's first thought. "No . . . *worse*," she moaned as she slapped the paper down on the table.

On the top, in bold letters, the page read ABIGAIL ADAMS JUNIOR HIGH SCIENCE FAIR.

"This is, like, the ultimate tragedy."

Matt muffled a burst of laughter. "Is that a fact? If I remember correctly, didn't you tell me just last week that *Romeo and Juliet* was the ultimate tragedy?"

"I mean in my own life, Matthew." Maeve rolled her eyes, but secretly loved how Matt was joking with her . . . maybe even . . . *flirting*? She wasn't positive, but she made a mental note to ask the BSG later. "We both know that science stuff is hard enough for me as it is. But did you read this thing? It says I need to do an *experiment. An experiment*! Who do they think I am? Albert Armstrong?"

"You mean, Albert Einstein?"

Maeve flipped her hair. "*Whatever*. Science and drama girls like me do not mix. Well, most of the time, anyway," she added, not wanting to sound like a complete doof in front of this dreamy college boy. "I mean, really, what am I supposed to do an experiment on—if my hair looks better curly or straight? Please."

Matt leaned his head forward and sighed. Maeve wondered if she had gone too far, even for her. But Matt popped back up again and said, "Okay, Maeve, chill time. This is totally doable. First of all, girls can be great at science, and if you don't believe me, then you've got to go to the Sally Ride Science Festival for girls. It's at MIT this weekend and it is going to be seriously interesting."

Before Maeve even had a chance to say, *More science? I don't think so,* . . . Matt had taken a brochure out of his bag. "Check it out."

Maeve expected to see snapshots of a drab gymnasium full of boring-looking posters and homemade volcanoes. But the pictures of the fair were outdoors, right by the Charles River overlooking downtown Boston. There were girls everywhere and huge booths filled with colors. *This doesn't look like a boring science festival to me,* Maeve thought, looking at Matt suspiciously. There was even a close-up that showed a group of girls trying on lip gloss.

"My friend Bailey has been working on it for weeks. It's going to be totally crazy—girls come from all over for this."

Even though Maeve knew that the Massachusetts Institute of Technology was one of the most famous universities in the world, she gave a little wave with her hand, as if that would make the whole science fair thing just disappear. "No offense, Matt . . . I could understand people coming from far and wide for a movie premiere—like they did with *Titanic,* or like, *Harry Potter.* But honestly . . . a crowd for a science festival?" Her voice dropped to a whisper. "Doesn't that seem just a little . . . nerdy?"

Matt rubbed his temples. Maeve had seen her mother do this thousands of times . . . usually when Maeve's bedroom reached a messiness level her mom called "the danger zone."

"Well, from what Bailey told me, this festival is going to be anything *but* nerdy. There are booths and workshops where you can try awesome stuff, like making a bracelet based on your DNA. And a workshop where you can design your own lip gloss flavor."

Jewelry and makeup? Maeve liked the sound of that. And her own self-designed lip gloss called Pink Satin Princess— she liked the sound of that even better! *But DNA? . . .* that sounded complicated.

"Plus, there's going to be food there. Hey, Maeve, tell you what. Why don't we go together this Saturday? It'll be a great way for you to see how science can be fun, and maybe even inspire you to come up with an idea for your own experiment for the Abigail Adams Science Fair. Think about it."

"Huh?" Maeve had totally zoned out after Matt had uttered the words, "together this Saturday." Could it be true? She had just been asked out by the cutest college boy in the entire world—or at least in Boston, for sure. She looked up to answer with a confident yes, but then became lost in his big, beautiful blue eyes. They got her every time! "Yabba I-I-I mean, *yes*, of course I'll go with you, Matt."

"Cool. I bet you'll see some science that'll be really interesting to you."

"I doubt it," a skeptical Maeve blurted out before she remembered that Matt had asked her to be his date for the festival. She hoped he wouldn't change his mind now.

But Matt didn't even seem to notice her lack of enthusiasm. Instead he started going on and on about alternative energies, global warming, and his friend Bailey's organic fertilizer. Then all of a sudden his eyes widened.

"Hey, I have a great idea. You should ask your friends, you know, the BSG, if they want to come along too. They have to come up with their science projects too, right?"

Maeve felt that sick feeling—the one that meant something wonderful was oh-so-quickly slipping away. If her friends were there, it just wouldn't be the same! "But you're my tutor," she sputtered. "You don't want to have to tutor five girls at once, do you?"

Matt laughed. "I don't mind at all. The more the merrier. Besides, it won't be like tutoring so much as us hanging out like friends. You'll get to meet Bailey. And there's going to be a DJ there."

Phew, Maeve thought. He was just trying to be nice to her and make her feel more comfortable. That had to be a little bit romantic—at least according to an article she'd read in *Teen Beat* magazine.

"Okay Matt, you have *got* to hear this song," Maeve told him, trying to keep their conversation on music, far away from science. "It's by Jake Axle and it's called 'I Am Rubber, You Are Glue' and it's so hot that like, seriously, I'm afraid smoke is going to start coming out of my iPod!" Maeve hopped up to play the song, but she felt a tug on the back of her sweater.

"Hold on one second there, Maeve. We need to make a dent in your math homework."

"But, but, Jake Axle . . . ," Maeve pleaded. She gave him her best *I'll be so good if you do* look. "Please, Matt. *Pleeeeease*?"

"Tell you what, if we still have time after you finish your math homework, then we'll listen to your hot Jake Axle song." Matt put his hand out for Maeve to shake. "Deal?"

Maeve smiled and grabbed his hand. "Deal!" Her heart did a little flip-flop. She couldn't believe she was actually touching the hand of Matt the Adorable!

Concentrating on the rest of the lesson was definitely challenging, but Maeve did her best to focus. She was positive that once Matt saw the moves she had choreographed, he would definitely be impressed. She flipped open her laptop and scrolled through her calendar, searching for today's homework assignments. Because she was dyslexic, her teachers let her bring a laptop to class to help with writing and spelling. Fortunately that meant she could also use the laptop to keep track of her very busy life, which *unfortunately* seemed to always include hours of homework.

After what seemed like forever and a half, she finished the exercises assigned in her textbook. "*Done!*" Maeve cried at the end of twenty minutes of pre-algebra torture. She dropped her head on the tabletop for a half-second, jumped to her feet, and ran over to the CD player. The room thumped with the beat of drums, electric guitars, and a keyboard. Maeve folded her hands across her chest and froze until Jake's honey voice started crooning:

> *You and I, we were two birds oh so fly*
> *Going to awards shows, me so proud to be your guy*
> *But then you broke my heart like Humpty Dumpty*
> *on that wall*
> *I felt so hurt that I ever had to fall*
> *But I am bouncy rubber, baby*
> *You are sticky glue—sticky icky*
> *That stuff you said about me once*
> *I'm bouncing back on you*

Maeve was thrilled as she got her groove going in perfect step to Jake Axle's new number one single. At the end of the song Maeve spun around and struck a pose in an almost-perfect imitation of Bedazzle, whose number one videos had

the absolute best choreography, in Maeve's professional opinion. She had been practicing the singer's signature move for
months now. *Am I ready to star in my own music video or what?*
she thought proudly, looking up at Matt and wiping a tiny
pearl of sweat off her forehead.

"Mix-Master-Curl in the houuuuse!" Matt cheered. He
put two fingers in his mouth and sounded a loud whistle.
"That was off the hook, Maeve. How did you remember that
whole routine?"

Maeve, who usually had answers for everything, could
only shrug. She was thrilled that Matt recognized her mad
dance skills. She thought her heart might skip a beat!

"Okay, Maeve, now for the really big announcement.
You managed to get every answer correct. I'm very proud
of you."

"Really?" Maeve asked, totally surprised. "But I'm terrible in math, so how did I get all of those problems right?"

"It's just like dancing, Maeve," Matt told her wisely. "You
gotta work at that, right? I mean, you must have practiced
that routine for hours. The more you practice, the better you
get. Same with math." He grabbed his book bag and slung
it over his shoulder. "I gotta go, but we're on for Saturday,
right?" he asked. Maeve managed a nod as she started shuf-
fling through her closet in her head—planning an outfit was
sort of a gut reaction. "Great! I'll text you with the times and
stuff. Check it out with your friends and your mom. Take it
easy, Mix-Master-Curl!" Matt called over his shoulder as he
headed out the door.

Sitting cross-legged on the kitchen floor, Maeve's heart
was still beating like crazy. *Mix-Master-Curl . . .* She wrapped

a strand of her curly red hair around her finger, then jumped up to look in the mirror. Lucky for her, the frizz attack was under control today. She wondered if Matt liked red hair. Some boys at school made fun of it. But luckily, she had Katani, the style queen, to reassure her: "Luxuriate in your red curls, Maeve. They're distinctive."

"Hey, Maeve? Guess what?" It was Sam. Now he was in his full Army uniform. Maeve had to admit—he made an impressive little Army dude. She let go of her hair and watched it spring back into a perfect banana curl.

"What?" She turned to smile at her precious little brother.

"I'm going too!"

And before Maeve had a chance to scream "*Nooooooooo!*" her pesty little brother was gone.

2

Fair Weather

*A*very Madden zipped over to the BSG lunch table with a plastic tray teetering in her hands. "Happy Friday to me! Spaghetti and meatballs today! You gotta love it. That's like a million times better than tuna fish surprise. Who's with me?" Avery held out her hand for her friends to slap her five but nobody was paying attention. They were all staring at Maeve. Charlotte's mouth was open so wide that Avery worried her jaw might just hit the cafeteria floor. "Okay, what's the soap opera today, BSG?" she asked.

Isabel looked up at Avery with wide eyes. "Maeve says she has . . . a date."

Maeve sat beside Isabel, munching away on a meatball and beaming from ear to ear. She explained, "Yes. A date with a real, live college guy."

Katani rolled her eyes. "It's just her tutor, Matt. He's taking her to some science thing at MIT. Trust me, girlfriend, science festival plus your college-age math tutor does not equal a date."

Charlotte, the writer and the most imaginative of the group, held up her spoon to object. "Wait a minute there, Kgirl. Haven't you ever heard of a thing called *chemistry*? That's science too, after all."

"That's funny, Char." Isabel giggled.

"Well, a girl can dream. Why don't you guys come along?" Maeve suggested. "Matt asked me to invite you all so you can get some ideas for your science fair projects, too. Wasn't that darling of him?"

"Okay, Maeve, if he invited your friends, not no way, not no how is this a date," a blunt Avery told her. "Even I know that." But Maeve, lost in her own romantic fantasies, hardly gave her friends' suspicions any thought.

Charlotte spooled a few strands of spaghetti around on her fork and commented to no one in particular, "What do you think, guys? A science festival could be fun. I saw a flier about the Sally Ride Science one at Montoya's yesterday, and it looks wicked."

"Wicked, huh?" Avery gave Charlotte a joking nudge. "Looks like some of our cool Boston lingo is finally rubbing off on our world traveler."

Charlotte had lived all over the world, including Australia, Africa, and Paris. When her father landed a job at a college back in their home town of Boston, Charlotte quickly realized that she felt right at home—especially now, with her new best friends, the BSG. But the funny Boston expressions . . . well, they still felt a little weird coming out of her mouth. She was sure her face had turned watermelon pink. *Did I sound completely goofy saying "wicked"?* she wondered.

"Count me out, BSG. I've got my pick-up soccer game on

Saturday. Nothing messes with my soccer," Avery said with a grin.

"Well, I really want to see the experiments on alternative energy, like wind. Alternative energy is the hot thing, you know. Imagine living in a house powered entirely by wind or water. . . ." Charlotte nodded emphatically.

"Whoa," Isabel said. "That sounds totally sci-fi! How does that work?"

All the girls looked interested . . . except Maeve, who was worried that the conversation was about to get a little too science-y for her taste. She tried to steer things back to her own hot topic—a certain dreamy, blue-eyed tutor.

"Forget alternative energy, Char. This festival is going to be positively *dripping* with handsome college guys." Maeve fanned her face with her hand.

Avery made a gagging noise and Katani, who looked totally annoyed, blurted out, "Girlfriend, get real. We're twelve. I barely have time to look for a boyfriend in the seventh grade."

"I know, I know." Maeve pouted. Katani could be such a bummer sometimes. "Can't I just crush on him for a while?" she added defensively.

"You can crush on whoever you want, but boys shouldn't be the reason you go to a science festival," Katani said.

"Earth to Maeve," Charlotte interrupted and reached over to grab Maeve's arm. "I hate to break it to you, but this festival is *girls only* . . . fifth to eighth graders."

"Forget the date debate, you all," Isabel piped up, through a mouthful of crunchy lettuce. "Charlotte is right. This could be a fun thing to check out."

"I mean, I've wanted to go to the holography exhibit at the MIT museum ever since I moved to Boston," she added. "Art in 3D? Does it get any *cooler*?" Isabel, the resident artist of the BSG, was constantly awing students with her funny cartoons in *The Sentinel*—the AAJH school paper.

Avery suddenly stood up with a now-empty lunch tray. "Looks like I've done enough damage here," she said, patting her stomach. "You ladies can continue this date debate . . . I'm headed outside to the court . . . the b-ball court!" She turned to sprint her way to the tray depository.

"Wait!" Maeve cried. "Ave, did you know that MIT has one of the biggest college sports programs in the country?" Katani raised an eyebrow dubiously, but Maeve protested, "No, it's totally true. Matt told me. *And* you all might be interested to know that MIT has a whole system of underground tunnels . . . they might be pretty cool to explore."

Avery slowly turned around. "Excuse me, did somebody just say sports and underground tunnels?" Maeve nodded her head up and down, sending her long curls into a vibrant bounce. "Okay, now I'm interested. Count me in! The soccer boys at the park will just have to manage without my superior talents." Avery laughed as she ran off.

Katani tossed the end of her bright yellow, handmade scarf over her shoulder and answered, "Well, if you all are going, I'm in, too. I'll just have to make sure that Patrice can stay with Kelley while I'm gone. You know Kelley. Large crowds and underground tunnels would be a definite recipe for disaster." Katani loved her older sister Kelley—they did tons of after-school activities together and even shared a room. But having a sister with autism meant that Katani had a lot of extra responsibilities . . . and needed extra patience. Katani didn't mind. Sometimes, though, it was nice to get a break.

"So then it's settled!" Maeve announced. She stood up and, all jazzy-like, stretched out her arms and wiggled her fingers. "Official BSG outing slash Maeve Kaplan-Taylor sorta kinda maybe date with an adorable tutor." Avery let out an audible groan as Maeve went on, "This Saturday morning we'll meet at the T stop on Beacon Street. Sally Ride Science Festival, make way for the BSG!"

"Hey, I have an idea: What about roping in Scott and Elena Maria?" Avery exclaimed, skidding back into her seat at the table. "It's our chance to get them together."

Scott was Avery's older brother; Elena Maria was Isabel's older sister. They were both in high school, both very cool, both loved cooking, and both—the girls suspected—secretly had crushes on each other. Elena Maria was dating this other guy, Jimmy, but Isabel knew for a fact that her sister wasn't very happy with the situation. Jimmy wasn't what she'd call the most thoughtful kind of guy. And Scott and Elena Maria had been amazing about helping the girls this year. They were the ones who had lent a hand to make all the delicious food for the BSG bake sale when they needed to raise money for their trip out west.

"That's an awesome idea!" Isabel agreed. "They would probably be happy to take us to the Science Festival . . . they could be chaperones, too. Especially if it means an excuse to hang out with each other . . . right?"

"Totally," Maeve agreed. "Let's chat online tonight and firm up the details."

Suddenly, out of the corner of her eye, Katani noticed two super-trendy outfits moving toward them. Even while she was relaxing, her fashion radar was always on. "Make way for trouble," she murmured.

"Yikes!" Avery cried. "QOM at one o'clock."

Anna McMasters and Joline Kaminsky, a.k.a the Queens of Mean, were headed toward the BSG table. Anna looked like she was bursting with her usual ill will. The QOM were social climbers to the max, with a nasty habit of making fun of basically everybody while whispering and giggling—even during class. Charlotte dubbed them the "whisperers" when she first moved to Brookline. Katani gave them an A plus for their fashion efforts (she said they were funky and coura-geous), but gave their personalities a D minus minus.

"Hold the phone," Anna squealed as she click-clacked her way to the table with a bright pink smile pasted to her face. "Did I actually hear you BSG saying that you were going to a science festival this weekend?"

"And just when I thought that your little group of friends couldn't get any pathetic-er," Joline added.

"I don't think 'pathetic-er' is a word, Joline," Charlotte informed her—with her own satisfied smile. "Which you would know, if you had paid attention to the vocabulary sec-tion Ms. R assigned us last week."

Anna snorted. "Well, excuse us if we're not, like, super-nerds like you BSG, or whatever."

Joline leaned over and whispered something to Anna, and the two of them immediately burst out laughing.

"Major point, Jo," Anna said conspiratorially. "My cool friend here just reminded me that we have plans for this weekend. Plans that don't involve being ultra-geeks 24/7. Plans that are so cool that you wouldn't even understand if we told you in English."

"What's that supposed to mean?" Isabel muttered to Avery.

"That we don't speak Crazy . . . the native language of the Queens of Mean?" Avery answered.

As Avery and Isabel shared their own little giggle, Anna and Joline strutted away, swinging their shoulders and arms back and forth like they were trying to walk down a fashion runway. When they passed Avery, Anna stopped and suddenly something round and very blue began to bulge out of her lips. It grew bigger and bigger. It was certainly bigger than any bubble gum bubble that Avery had ever seen before, and she considered herself sort of an expert on gum. Just when she thought Anna's bubble was going to float up to the cafeteria ceiling from Anna's lips, Anna flicked out her tongue, snapped the gum, and slurped it into her mouth with one gasp. It was incredible really—especially since she managed to get not even a tiny fleck of gum on her face.

"Enjoy the geek fest, dweebettes." Anna smirked. With that, she and Joline flitted away.

"I really can't take those two," grumbled Charlotte, who hardly ever had a negative thing to say about anybody.

"Me either!" Avery exclaimed. "But I really want to know where Anna got that ri-*donc*-ulous blue gum. I've never seen anything like it! Do you think it might be extraterrestrial?"

"Translation?" Maeve demanded.

"Extraterrestrial means from another planet. Like Martians or aliens," Charlotte explained. Char was the BSG resident word nerd—and proud of it.

Isabel shuddered. "Gosh, I hope not. But being from another planet could answer a lot of unsolved mysteries about those two girls."

The BSG shared a laugh as they gathered their trays and made their way back to class.

Growing Pains (in the Neck)

That night, Maeve was at her dad's apartment trying to figure out what to wear to the science festival. She was still getting used to having parents who were separated. It was hard, going from a family where both parents were always there at the beginning and end of the day to switching from apartment to apartment every other weekend. And it always made her a little sad when she didn't see her dad during the week. The whole separated-parents thing was just so complicated, she thought with a sigh. And annoying—*like, how am I ever supposed to put together the perfect Science Festival outfit when I don't even have all my clothes in one place?*

In her head, Maeve had it all planned out. She wanted to wear her perfect pink puffy-cap-sleeve blouse with her favorite pair of Audrey Hepburn-inspired, skinny, black Capri pants. Unfortunately, her perfect blouse was perfectly clean, perfectly ironed, and hanging perfectly on a hanger in the closet . . . at her mother's apartment.

At least she had packed her back-up blouse, the one she wore all the time back in sixth grade, and hoped it still fit. She pulled her arms into the sleeves. *Phew*—they were still long enough. But when she started to button up the front, things felt all weird. She looked at herself in the mirror and shook her head. The blouse felt way too small, but her pants from sixth grade still fit.

Suddenly, Maeve heard a knock at the door. "It's me, honey. Can I come in?" called Mr. Taylor.

"No! I'm changing!" Maeve cried, and without even thinking about it, folded her arms across her chest.

"Well, come out when you're ready," her dad told her. "I want to find out what your final plans are for this Science Festival outing."

"Okay, Dad, gimme a minute." Maeve furiously tore off her once-favorite blouse and, wearing just a white tank-top with her jeans, stared at her reflection in the full length mirror. She studied herself from every angle, feeling puzzled. She hadn't outgrown her pants from sixth grade yet. Was it possible to go up a size on one part of your body but not another?

Suddenly, the truth hit her like a lighting bolt. She felt her face flush as she realized what the difference was. She, Maeve Kaplan-Taylor, was in desperate need of . . . a *bra*!

Maeve crossed her arms and threw herself onto the bean-bag in the corner to think this over. At that moment, more than ever before, Maeve wished divorces, separations, and different homes were illegal or something. She definitely needed her Mom right now—talking to her dad about bras was absolutely, positively out of the question. So totally weird it made her shudder just to think about it. But she wouldn't be seeing her mom before the Festival tomorrow, so what could she do?

Maeve resolved to wear a striped pink sweater with her jeans instead, and sadly folded her old favorite blouse and placed it back in her bureau. This was a milestone moment for Maeve, who never folded anything—much to über-organized Katani's utter dismay.

She shook her head to clear it and decided that it would probably be a smart idea to actually have plans to talk to her dad about, so she signed online hoping that the BSG would be online too.

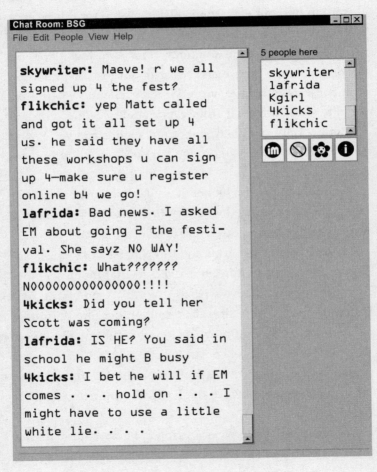

skywriter: Maeve! r we all signed up 4 the fest?
flikchic: yep Matt called and got it all set up 4 us. he said they have all these workshops u can sign up 4—make sure u register online b4 we go!
lafrida: Bad news. I asked EM about going 2 the festival. She sayz NO WAY!
flikchic: What??????? NOOOOOOOOOOOOOOOO!!!!
4kicks: Did you tell her Scott was coming?
lafrida: IS HE? You said in school he might B busy
4kicks: I bet he will if EM comes . . . hold on . . . I might have to use a little white lie. . . .

Chat Room: BSG

File Edit People View Help

skywriter: Avery!!! Lies will make your nose grow U know

4kicks: lol. So what? I could use a little growing. brb, I'm going to ask him now. . . .

lafrida: + it's for the good of science and mankind!!!!

flikchic: and for the good of love . . . sigh

lafrida: chillax, love muffin

Kgirl: u r 2 much Maeve!

4kicks: Success!! He's in. He said he might want to check out MIT to GO TO one day. Yeah right. Lol!!! Now ask your sis, Iz. . . .

lafrida: now cross your fingers . . . I'll go work on Elena. . . . brb

flikchic: Im crossing my TOES

4kicks: Im putting on my lucky socks!

skywriter: Im wearing my lucky jacket . . . OMG what else can I do?

5 people here

skywriter
lafrida
Kgirl
4kicks
flikchic

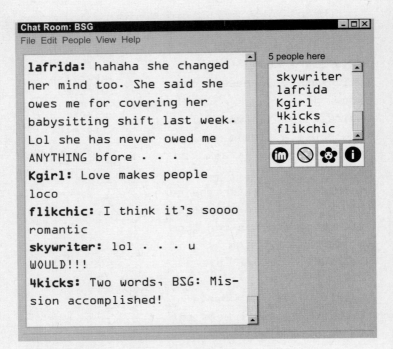

Chat Room: BSG

File Edit People View Help

lafrida: hahaha she changed her mind too. She said she owes me for covering her babysitting shift last week. Lol she has never owed me ANYTHING bfore . . .

Kgirl: Love makes people loco

flikchic: I think it's soooo romantic

skywriter: lol . . . u WOULD!!!

4kicks: Two words, BSG: Mission accomplished!

5 people here

skywriter
lafrida
Kgirl
4kicks
flikchic

CHAPTER

3

A Terrible T-Party

Isabel couldn't believe that she was awake before noon on a Saturday, and what was even more unbelievable, that she was awake before noon to learn about science. But she was excited to get Elena Maria together with Scott Madden, and who could pass up a 3D holograph exhibit? Actually, she had been lying in bed for at least an hour now, thinking about 3D bird images and waiting for Elena Maria to get out of the bathroom.

When she realized it was getting late, Isabel finally rolled out from under her squishy comforter. It took her all of two seconds to throw on a pair of comfy green sweats and her current favorite T-shirt—one with a beautiful parrot on it saying, "Polly want a little piece and quiet at the Boston Public Library." Katani found it at a thrift shop and got it for Isabel, who loved birds and art with equal passion.

She went and knocked on the bathroom door. "Are you ready to go yet, Miss Elena?"

"Almost!" Elena Maria hollered back.

"Almost?" Isabel was beginning to get worried. She really didn't want to be late to meet the BSG at the T stop. Isabel packed everything she needed for the fair, which was her sketchbook and pencil. Her art supplies were really all she needed to go anywhere. Then she straightened up her side of the room and made her bed. When she was done, she marched back to the bathroom and pounded on the door. "Elenaaaaaa! C'mon! This isn't the Grammys."

The door creaked opened, and Elena Maria popped her head out. "I'm having such a bad hair day. Would you look at this?" Elena held up a strand of her long, wavy, dark brown hair, with a look of dismay on her face.

Isabel couldn't believe her sister. "Are you kidding me? Elena, your hair, as usual, looks perfect. And are you serious? Eye makeup? At nine in the morning? We're not going to a party, *mi hermana*."

Elena Maria shrugged. "Well . . . I just thought . . ."

Isabel knew exactly what her sister thought. Elena Maria's cheeks were bright pink—and it wasn't the blush she was wearing. "You look awesome, Elena. But you're totally going to be the most dressed up girl at this thing."

But when they arrived at the train, Isabel saw that she was wrong—her sister was definitely not the most dressed-up girl attending the Sally Ride Science Festival. That prize had to go to (she should have known) the one—the only— Miss Maeve Kaplan-Taylor.

"Yoo-hoo! Martinez sisters! Over here!" Maeve waved her hand in the air, jangling the many charms on her bracelet.

Despite the minor snag in her ensemble plan the night before, Maeve was extremely proud of her final selection, which she deemed oh-so-college-y. She was wearing her favorite flared jeans that fit her just right with a soft pink sweater and a pink and scarlet plaid wool blazer. Though it had taken her nearly an hour to transform her famous red curls into a sleek, shiny, straight 'do, Maeve thought it was definitely worth the effort. She topped off the whole look with a little raspberry cap slightly tilted to the side, a leather briefcase her mother had saved from the eighties, and a pair of non prescription pink tortoise shell glasses.

The rest of the BSG watched Isabel stifle a giggle as she took in Maeve's totally over-the-top outfit.

"What do you think?" Maeve threw her arms in the air. "Am I college-prep, or what?"

It took all the strength Isabel could muster to reply, "Absolutely."

"Thanks! Plus, this briefcase doubles as a purse. Genius, right?" Maeve huddled the girls together and whispered, "And these glasses . . . aren't real, you know."

Katani shook her head. "Well, no kidding, girlfriend! I think we'd all know at this point if you wore glasses."

Charlotte adjusted her own *real* glasses and cleared her throat. "Ahem. Too bad you can't be as lucky as me to be born this way!"

"I wish I was!" Maeve exclaimed. "Glasses are soooo *in* right now, Char. They make you look ultra-sophisticated. I found these puppies at Think Pink after school yesterday. You gals have to swear on your lives you won't tell anyone they're fake!" she begged.

Even Katani and Avery, who both thought Maeve's romantic fantasies could be way too intense sometimes, couldn't help laughing. "You know, the thing about being friends with Maeve," Katani informed an awestruck Elena Maria, "is that life is always in full color."

Elena Maria smiled. "I can see that," she said. Then, turning pinker and speaking softer, she mumbled, "Hey, Scott."

Scott pulled out his iPod earphones, grunted a quick, "'Sup," and quickly replaced the earphones.

Elena Maria took the lid off a shoebox she was holding. "I made some of my chocolate and cinnamon spice cookies. I hope you like them as much as my salsa . . . you know, the one I made for the bake sale?"

"Huh?" Scott took out his earphones again. "Oh, sweet. Thanks, Elena." He took a cookie and went right back to listening to his music. The BSG gratefully helped themselves to the cookies, but despite the girls' excitement over the delicious treats, Isabel noticed that her sister looked majorly disappointed.

"So, so stupid," Elena Maria murmured to herself.

Avery glanced at Scott pointedly, but he was totally immersed in grooving to his tunes. "Don't worry, you two," Maeve whispered, looping her arms over her friends' shoulders. "That's part of the 'Secret Language of Boys.' I read all about it in *Teen Beat*. It said the less that comes out of his mouth, the *more* he likes the girl. Luckily, we females are *much* more advanced."

Avery, who spent way more time playing sports with dudes then reading crush articles about them, was surprisingly irritated at her big brother's behavior. "The least he could do is talk to her like a normal person! Is that too much to ask?"

Charlotte, Maeve, Isabel, and Katani looked at one another and answered at the same time, "*Yes!*"

"Besides, it could be worse. At least your brother *attempts* to be cool," Maeve complained. "Mine still thinks that cool means dressing up in weird costumes and making potions out of pickle juice and shaving cream. Can you believe Sam actually *wanted* to go to this science festival? Like, for *fun*. I told him it's for girls but he still wanted to go. Seriously, I had to sneak out of the house this morning while he was in the bathroom. It was a way close call." Maeve took a mirror out of her briefcase and applied sparkly gloss to her lips.

"Um, Maeve?" Katani gently elbowed her friend.

"One sec," Maeve said, studying her reflection so intently that she neglected to notice the station wagon pulling to a stop beside her.

"I am *very* disappointed in you, young lady!" scolded a deep voice from within the car.

Maeve didn't even have to turn around to know who it was. Her face turned pale as she weakly uttered, "Dad?"

"We made it! We made it!" Sam cheered. "Houston, we *don't* have a problem!" He popped out of the passenger seat and skipped right over to Maeve.

Dressing up must be part of the Kaplan-Taylor DNA, Charlotte thought, fighting the urge to grin. Much to Maeve's horror, Sam had chosen to sport a bright blue *Star Trek* costume—the one he had worn for the last two Halloweens in a row—complete with plastic pointed ears.

"Good morning, girls!" Mr. Taylor greeted the BSG, back to his normal, cheerful self. "Oh, and good morning, *boy*," he added goofily, saluting Scott Madden. "I thought you might need a little Spock to help you navigate your way through the world of science, boldly going where no BSG has gone before . . . ,"

"Daaaaaaad, the Festival's for girls," Maeve breathed through clenched teeth.

"Live long and prosper," Sam greeted Charlotte, holding up one hand with the fingers spread apart in the middle.

Charlotte covered her heart with two hands and mouthed "*He's so cute!*" to Maeve.

Maeve clearly did not agree. "Dad, you can't be serious," she moaned.

"Do I look serious?" Mr. Taylor asked. With his bushy eyebrows and out-of-control curly hair, Maeve thought her father looked anything *but* serious, though she knew better than to say that now. "You are babysitting, Maeve. I checked with the festival people, and little brothers are welcome as long as someone is responsible for them."

"But, Dad, it's supposed to be my special day with Ma—I mean, learning about science and stuff. Not the day I have to supervise my Martian slash brother."

"Hey! Who you calling a Martian? I'm a *Vulcan . . . duh!*" Sam thwacked his head with his palm in frustration.

"I'll keep an eye on him, Maeve . . . if you want," Charlotte volunteered. As an only child, Charlotte often wondered what it would be like to have siblings. Sure, her friends complained sometimes, but she saw how much fun all the kids in big families had together. And if she *did* have a brother, she secretly wished he would be just like Sam—school-obsessed and proud of it . . . the way that she was.

"That would be wonderful, Charlotte!" Mr. Taylor said with a grateful smile.

Charlotte nodded, glancing fondly at Sam. "Totally."

"Of course, I would pay you as a regular babysitter," he added. "Five bucks an hour."

"Five bucks? Really?" Charlotte squeaked with a smile. She was saving money for a journal she'd seen with a pretty purple suede cover.

"*Really?*" Maeve squeaked with a frown. Now she was feeling totally guilty and annoyed. As the big sister, it was her job to take care of Sam. She didn't want her friends to have to deal with him, and she *definitely* didn't want her dad to have to shell out cash for it. "Char, you really don't have to—" Maeve started.

"No, it'll be fun!" Charlotte said enthusiastically. "It's just a good thing I didn't bring Marty. Then I'd have two little pups to look after!" she joked as she tousled Sam's shaggy hair. Marty was the adorable little pooch that belonged to all the BSG but lived with Charlotte and her father. It had been doggie love at first sight when the BSG rescued him from a garbage can.

Maeve could hardly believe her eyes when Sam laughed along with Charlotte's joke. If Maeve had called him a "pup," he would have been telling on her to their parents in two seconds! *What disloyalty!* She guessed Sam and Charlotte had some kind of brainiac connection she couldn't understand, which only made her feel worse for not living up to her big-sisterly duties.

The T arrived just as Mr. Taylor was getting back into the car. "Thank you so much, Charlotte!" He waved and restarted the noisy station wagon. "Good-bye . . . Maeve . . . Sam, be good for Charlotte." And then he was off.

Feeling somewhat dejected, Maeve took her time boarding the train. As she climbed the stairs behind Scott, she wondered what her father had meant by that last part. Was he just saying bye? He wasn't telling *her* to be good, too . . . was he? Didn't her dad realize that she was practically a teenager? After all, she was definitely ready to start wearing a bra. What she needed right now was to talk to a real-live teenager, someone who would know for sure if she, Maeve Kaplan-Taylor, was a mature teenager too.

The gang took their seats on the crowded train. Elena Maria thoughtfully scooted next to the window, leaving one empty seat. And since Scott was the only person still standing, she was pretty sure he was going to end up right where she wanted him—right next to her. Maybe once they started chatting he would get more comfortable and start acting like her friend again.

Scott scanned the train and immediately spotted Elena Maria and the empty seat beside her. He took out his earphones and nervously began, "Hey, Elena, do you mind if I—"

"'Scuse me, Scott!" Maeve sang, squeezing through the crowd. "Yowch! Make way, please. Coming through." Maeve shot past Scott and let out a huge sigh as she collapsed next to Elena Maria. "Gosh, that was a close call! I have some serious issues to discuss and the only other open seat was next to Katani."

"Um, Maeve, wouldn't you like to discuss your 'serious issues' with Katani? She *is* one of your best friends . . . ," Elena Maria suggested.

Maeve shook her head. "I can't talk to Katani about these things. I need to talk to an older woman. Hey, Scott, you can grab the seat next to Kgirl if you want."

"Sure . . . whatever," Scott mumbled. Katani didn't say a word as Scott sat down, but continued to flip through the magazine in her lap.

"Whatcha reading?" he asked, attempting to be friendly.

"*Fashion Plate*," she replied without looking up.

"Cool. Oh, right, Avery said that you were, like, wicked into clothes."

"Fashion," Katani corrected. "Clothes are just clothes. Clothes are what *you* wear. But fashion . . . well, *fashion* is art." Katani hoped she didn't sound rude, but she really didn't appreciate being interrupted when she was in the middle of creative inspiration. All she wanted to do on the train ride was read the latest issue of *Fashion Plate* and think about the future fashion lines she would create someday, when she was a big-time designer.

"So, uh, are you also into sports?" Scott asked.

Katani was now officially annoyed. Just because his sister Avery was a total sports nut did not mean that *she* was. "Not really," Katani answered. "Why?"

"Oh, well, I've seen your sister Patrice on the basketball court. She's amazing! I figured it must run in the family," Scott offered with a friendly smile.

"It doesn't," Katani informed him. If there was one thing that really got under her skin, it was being compared to her older sisters, Patrice and Candice, who were both exceptional athletes. Though Katani was tall and slim like her older sisters, she always felt like a total galumph on the basketball court. She hoped that people could see beyond her lack of sports talent to the future businesswoman and fashionista extraordinaire that she was inside.

Scott now was glad to turn on his iPod—though he wished he had *not* had it on before . . . back outside the train with Elena Maria. He had a funny feeling that he acted like a total dweeb when she offered him those cookies, which were delicious. Not to mention how pretty she looked. He tried to be subtle as he turned around to catch a glimpse.

Unfortunately his view was blocked by one peppy redhead, who was vivaciously babbling, "So at first I thought, be natural, Maeve. Wear your hair curly. After all, it is your signature look, right? Then I thought, but straight 'n sleek is soooo hot right now. *And* I'll look way older. *And* Matt is in college, so older is good! Not like, *old* old, but like, *college* old, you know?"

"Uh-huh." Maeve noticed Elena Maria make eye contact with Scott and give him a shy smile. *Oops!* Maeve felt a little twinge of guilt as she realized that by sitting next to Elena Maria, she was keeping the two high school lovebirds apart. She *was* all for Scott and Elena Maria getting some face time. But they would have hours together at the festival, and this was an emergency—she would be seeing Matt in less than twenty minutes!

Meanwhile, Charlotte was finding Sam quite entertaining. She was surprised at how much he knew about outer space, especially for an eight-year-old. Charlotte herself was an astronomy buff, and she and Sam were having a fantastic time trying to outsmart each other with a game of constellation trivia. "What are Orion's hunting dogs named?" Charlotte challenged.

"Duh! Canis Major and Canis Minor. C'mon . . . gimme a hard one!"

Avery and Isabel were pleased that they snagged seats next to each other, but very disappointed with the Elena Maria/Scott situation. "You know, for someone who's obsessed with romance, I can't believe how clueless Maeve is!" Avery complained.

"I know!" Isabel agreed. "Scott and Elena Maria are soooo perfect for each other. This day is going to be a total waste of matchmaking efforts if we don't do something, and *fast*."

Isabel stretched her neck up and slyly observed her sister—batting her eyes in Scott's direction. And Scott, Isabel was relieved to see, was batting *his* eyes right back at Elena Maria. She slid back down in her seat, turned to Avery, and said with a soft giggle, "I have a feeling that Cupid has taken matters into his own hands."

CHAPTER

4

Yurt Alert!

Maeve was still chatting Elena Maria's ear off when the T screeched to a stop at the Kendall Square station. "And so first he's all like, 'Oh, Maeve, come to the Festival.' But then he's all like, 'Oh, you should bring your friends.' And I'm like, well, that's a little weird, right? But *then* he's like, 'We can chill.' So *now* I just have no idea *what* to think!"

Elena Maria was trying very hard to be patient, but Maeve's ridiculous fantasy about her tutor needed a serious reality check. "Maeve, think. I mean, Matt is way too old—"

"Shh!" Maeve suddenly grabbed Elena Maria's arm, *hard*. "He's coming over. Omigosh, omigosh. How do I look? Is my hat on straight?"

"Um . . . no . . ." Elena Maria started.

"Good," Maeve replied as she fanned her face with two hands. She quickly inspected her fellow BSGs and decided, smugly, that she definitely was dressed in the *most* sophisticated ensemble. She watched breathlessly as Matt made his way over to the group, adorable as ever, in a tattered, backwards Red Sox cap. She *did* feel a sliver of annoyance when she saw the light-colored jeans he was wearing. Stone-wash was so over at AAJH.

Matt saw the cluster of seventh grade girls waiting by the T stop at 10:00 a.m., just as he and Maeve had specified. He scanned the girls, trying to recall if these were all the BSG, since he had only met them a handful of times before. The short girl with black hair in a side ponytail practicing batting with an imaginary bat and ball—that had to be Avery. And the tall girl reading some sort of fashion magazine, Matt had a feeling, was Katani. He could spot Charlotte and Isabel, playing with Sam. The only thing was . . . Maeve wasn't there.

A girl with long, straight red hair spun around and gave a little wave. Matt blinked. "Whoa!"

Maeve stood there for a moment . . . a long moment. "Um, uh, 'sup?" she finally managed.

"Good thing the *female* of the species is so much more advanced!" Isabel giggled to Avery.

"I didn't recognize you there for a second, Maeve. Wow, way to break down the hydrogen bonds in your hair's cortex with ceramic plates and ionic technology!"

"Actually, I just used a hair straightener." Maeve ran her fingers through her smooth locks. She couldn't believe how well her plan was going. Matt was obviously captivated by the new look—Maeve 2.0—the undated version. *This is just how I would picture it if we were dating in, like, seven years or something. I would be shooting my first big movie—co-starring Caleb Tucker. Matt would be a world-famous doctor, getting out of the hospital after saving a baby's life. We'd meet here, by the T stop at the Charles River, and he'd sing to me—*

"Well, we should get a move on," Matt announced, clapping his hands together. "It's already pretty crowded." Maeve blinked her way back to reality, as Matt ushered the group in the right direction. "I'm glad you all came," Matt was saying. "I have some very cool stuff to show you. Before you all head off to the workshops you signed up for, there's an awesome street fair part of the festival that we can check out. There are some mind-blowing booths with stuff like robots you can control and the chemistry of food."

Isabel and Maeve exchanged looks—both girls were there for chemistry that had to do with hearts, not test tubes.

"Wait till you guys see the phytoplankton exhibit. When you see algae under a microscope, well, let's just say it's a miracle how beautiful scum can be," said Matt.

Isabel perked up a little at that comment. She *did* love looking at beautiful things. That was how she got her artistic inspiration.

"What about the tunnels?" asked Avery. "I definitely want to check out the other exhibits here, but Maeve told me there were tunnels, and I love tunnels. So . . . what's the deal?"

Matt chuckled. "When we're finished up with the festival, I'll take you on a guided tour of the tunnels. But for now, let's hit the street fair. Then I'm going to take you to see my friend Bailey's booth." Maeve wondered if Bailey would be as adorable as Matt. She doubted that was even possible.

"Welcome!" said a friendly volunteer, as the group approached the entrance. Maeve loved that the girl was rocking super-short, super-curly, dark brown hair.

SALLY RIDE
SCIENCE FESTIVAL

AT MIT!

FOR GIRLS IN GRADES 5 TO 8

FEATURING:

* A street fair with booths, food, and music!

* Fun workshops for girls!

* The chance to meet real scientists!

* Chaperones present!

* Workshops for parents and teachers, too!

PLUS ...

a special appearance by Sally Ride!

"Everyone's with me," Matt assured her. "We got special permission for this little guy." He indicated Sam.

"Sure, but the festivals are for girls in fifth to eighth grade," she said, looking at Scott and Elena Maria. "Sorry, guys."

Matt rubbed the back of his head, thinking, then said to Scott and Elena Maria, "Well, you two wanted to check out the campus anyway, right? Why don't you do that for a couple of hours and then meet us back here? Do you have a cell phone?"

Elena Maria nodded while Scott stared at his shoes nervously. Meanwhile, Isabel was beaming. She slapped Avery a secret high five behind Elena Maria's back. "Looks like they'll just *have* to spend two hours exploring a beautiful college together," she whispered to Avery, giggling.

"If Scott can work up the nerve to look at something other than the ground!" Avery whispered back, shaking her head.

"Okay, we'll see you back here when the festival is over," Matt instructed Elena Maria and Scott.

"Catch you later!" the BSG called out, with big smiles, as they watched their romance project walk away.

"All right, listen up, girls!" The volunteer got their attention. "Do you see the Sally Ride T-shirt I'm wearing? There are tons of other people in these T-shirts, just like me, and we're all here to help you. So if you have questions or need directions, just ask someone in one of these T-shirts."

"Now let's head in!" Matt exclaimed.

When she got a good look at the street fair scene, Maeve couldn't believe her eyes. At first, Maeve had had her doubts that the festival would be that cool an event. But now, she had to admit, it was totally looking like the happening place to be. There were girls everywhere, and all of them looked like they were having an absolute blast, running around with bags full of treasures and souvenirs they had collected from the various exhibits.

"Hey! What in the name of Einstein are *you guys* doing here?"

Maeve and the rest of the crew turned around. There was the AAJH seventh grade class president, Henry Yurt, wearing an over-sized T-shirt that read "My other car is a Proton Rocket."

"It's the Yurtmeister!" Maeve cried. She loved running into friends from school outside of school . . . especially when she was with a super-cute older boy. She hoped Henry would take note and report this incident back to the rest of his guy friends in their class. "We're here for the science festival, silly. That's my *friend* Matt." She pointed to Matt, who was looking at the next booth over. "He's showing us around. He's in *college*."

"How did you get in?" asked Katani, trying to bring the conversation away from Maeve-fantasyland and back to planet Earth. "I thought it was for girls only."

"My dad works here. He teaches zoology, and he helped organize this thing. Hey, wanna meet him? He's right over there." Henry Yurt pointed at a nearby booth.

The Yurtmeister led the way over to a booth with a banner hanging above it that said, DO YOU BELONG IN A ZOO? It was obviously a popular booth, because girls were swarming around it, laughing and chatting. In the middle of the booth was a short man with carrot-colored hair. He was a little on the bald side and also a grownup, but otherwise he was the spitting image of Henry Yurt. Avery noted that, like her, both Henry and his dad were "vertically challenged" — Avery-code for "short." But what really caught her attention was the tiny, furry creature sitting on Dr. Yurt's shoulders.

"And this little guy is on loan from the zoo, just for this special occasion," explained Henry's dad. "His name is Chewy."

"Like Chewbacca from *Star Wars*. Aaaaawesome!" exclaimed Sam. "Hey, Henry, your dad gets to take care of a monkey? That is so cool!" He gazed at Henry's dad like he was a superhero.

"That's no monkey, Sam," Avery corrected. "That little guy is a *lemur*. They're super-special because they only live in Madagascar. But monkeys and lemurs *are* both primates."

"Good for you, little lady." Yurt's dad pointed at Avery.

"Professor Yurtmeister! Duuuuude! You brought Chewy!" called a guy wearing a backwards baseball cap.

"What's up, my dawwwwgs?" Professor Yurt greeted his students.

Charlotte had to stifle a giggle. She'd seen her own dad trying to be cool around his students and knew exactly what was up. She turned to Maeve and whispered, "No matter how 'down with it' parents think they are, it never works."

"Hey, there, Li'l Yurt!" The guy with the baseball cap grinned, bending down to give Henry's hair a friendly rub. Avery always admired Henry's confidence: for a little dude, he had the self-respect of someone six feet tall. He totally embraced the nickname and attention. In no time at all, he had a crowd of college students surrounding him and his father, cracking up at the father-son comedians.

"You think we could get 'Li'l Yurt' to stick back at school?" asked Maeve.

"Maaaaaybe. All I have to say is, Yurt plus Yurt is a dynamite combination!" Avery told Isabel. Suddenly, something behind Isabel caught her eye. "Check it out: Make your own slime!" Avery shouted. "Let's go, Iz. It's kinda like an art project." The two girls took off to a nearby booth, which boasted that each girl could create her own custom made slime . . . with different colors and textures.

Katani took one look at the slime stand and her face turned pale. "No way is any kind of slime juice getting near this scarf," she vowed to Charlotte. "This material is 100 percent silk!"

"Fine by me," Maeve agreed, nervously brushing off her soft pink blazer.

"And me. I do not have a good track record with slimy stuff," Charlotte added. She scanned the scene around them and pointed at a booth. "Hey, look! A solar car display."

Sam started jumping up and down. "Solar cars are sweet, man!"

He may be smart, but he probably doesn't know what solar cars are. Maeve sniffed. She was miffed that Sam wasn't paying any attention to her at all. Suddenly, Charlotte was his favorite person in the world.

"That looks interesting," Katani agreed. In Maeve's opinion, electricity meant math, and math equaled total yawnfest, but at least at the solar booth thingy she wouldn't get any slime on her clothes.

The girls and Sam walked over to the booth, where a girl

with white-blonde hair was explaining what the big block sitting next to her was: a hydrogen cell that could power a car. "That's the H in H_2O," she told them. "Hydrogen is like the most abundant gas in the universe. In a process called fusion, two hydrogen atoms combine to form one helium atom, releasing energy as radiation. And best of all, enviro-fans—it's totally nonpolluting. Right now, it's expensive, but there are smart folks working on a hydrogen car that's more affordable.

"And now, the moment you've all been waiting for!" The girl whipped a black silk scarf off a small, shiny model sports car. The crowd oohed and ahhhed as the car drove around and around in a circle.

"This car is a hydromobile," the blonde girl explained.

"Gotta love the style," Maeve whispered to Katani and Charlotte.

"You know," Charlotte began, "my dad promised that if we buy a new car in a few months it will be a hybrid—a combo of electric and gas engines. I don't want to be driving a gas guzzler."

"A pink car," Maeve added and sighed. "All cars should be pink."

"Hey, what's that big crowd over there for?" asked Katani.

Indeed, a huge mass had formed at the booth beside them, and at the front Charlotte noticed something that nearly made her eyes pop out of her head. "You guys, it's—it's about *stars*! Meet a real live astronaut! I gotta—"

And with that, she was off, with Sam in tow. "I want to meet a real live astronaut too!" he shouted.

"C'mon, c'mon!" She laughed, eager to have her pint-sized partner in crime by her side.

"Take care of Sam!" Maeve shouted after Charlotte. Charlotte gave her a thumbs up as she swung Sam's hand into the air.

Maeve and Katani could barely keep up as Charlotte and Sam made their way through the crowd with the type of frenzy the girls had only seen Avery use during an intense game of basketball.

"A real astronaut!" Even Maeve was excited.

Katani read the sign more closely. "Maeve, that's not just any astronaut . . . that's Sally Ride herself—the first American woman to go into space!"

Maeve looked excitedly at Katani. "Should we follow?"

Katani shivered. "Girl, are you kidding me? Take a look at that monster line. I say we stay right here and wait for Charlotte to do her thing."

Maeve's eyes twinkled. "Or . . . head on over to our workshop? Matt said we'd get to make bracelets based on our DNA . . . whatever that is."

Katani checked her wristwatch and smiled. "Yep, it's almost time for the workshop to start. Let's go! FYI, DNA stands for deoxyribonucleic acid. It's basically your genes."

Maeve stared at Katani. Her friends were so smart. She started feeling like a loser-brain when all of a sudden she remembered that Thursday afternoon she'd gotten all her math problems correct. That made her stand a little taller as the girls strolled over to the volunteer holding a sign for their workshop.

On the other side of the festival, Avery and Isabel were in

a workshop that had them totally captivated by phytoplankton. Another college student, or as Avery insisted on calling her, "Genius MIT professor," was showing a captivated group all about how phytoplankton was crucial to the health of the ocean and how someday algae might even be a source of energy.

"I cannot believe that something that looks like pond scum can actually be a source for energy!" Avery remarked. "Just amazing."

After the workshop, Isabel wanted to know more. "I just can't believe how interesting these plants are under a microscope," said Isabel, her mind already ticking with how she could illustrate phytoplankton in her sketchbook.

"Excuse me, Professor Sullivan," Isabel started, reading the workshop leader's last name off her nametag.

"Actually, I'm just a grad student," the woman said with a kind laugh. "I hope I'll be Professor Sullivan one day! But for now, Emily is fine."

Isabel blushed. "Would I maybe be able to take some pamphlets with me about the um . . . phytoplankton?"

Emily laughed cheerfully. "Well, of course. That's what they're there for." Isabel began stuffing her (and Avery's) arms with all the free info she could find about phytoplankton.

Meanwhile, Matt had his hands full trying to collect the BSG.

"Katani! Maeve!" he huffed. "Great—I found you." Matt jogged over to the girls, who were proudly admiring their handcrafted DNA bracelets. Next to him were a grinning Sam and an excited-looking Charlotte Ramsey.

"You guys are not going to believe this." She held up her

journalism notebook. "I was almost late for my workshop, but I just couldn't pass up the opportunity to get *this*. Right here, smack on the front page. Look!"

Maeve leaned in and read slowly, "'Dear Charlotte. Reach for the stars. Sally K. Ride.' Whoa . . . you got Sally Ride's *autograph*?" In Maeve's world, anyone who was worthy of an autograph meant serious celebrity. She couldn't help feeling a tad jealous, although before today she honestly had no idea who Sally Ride was. Now she knew that she was someone very important.

"It's more than an autograph. It's called astro-encouragement. I'm definitely adding Sally Ride to my role model list—right next to Miss Pierce!" Miss Pierce, Charlotte's landlady who lived in the first floor apartment of the house they shared, was an astronomer who had worked on the design of the Hubble Space Telescope. She and Charlotte shared a passion for space and stars. "Sally Ride thinks that if I really wanted, I could be an astronaut someday, too!"

Maeve giggled. "If becoming a world-famous writer doesn't work out."

Katani shrugged and slung an arm around Charlotte's shoulder. "Hey, who knows . . . maybe she'll do both!"

Matt looked around anxiously and ran his fingers through his hair. "Four down, two to go . . ." he murmured through clenched teeth. "Where could your buddies be?"

"Well," Katani said thoughtfully, "I do know that Avery was pretty excited about seeing more environmental stuff."

Matt clapped his hands. "Okay—follow me."

Maeve wished Matt would be a little more concerned with getting some romantic alone time with her instead of always trying to locate the group, but she knew her brave tutor was only being his usual responsible self. Just being with him made Maeve feel more responsible, too. As they walked along, she offered her hand to her little brother. "Want to hold my hand, Sam?" she asked sweetly.

"Nope. Dad said Charlotte's my babysitter today, remember?" He stuck out his tongue at Maeve and slipped his hand into Charlotte's, pulling her ahead.

Maeve couldn't believe it. First Matt practically ignored her, and now she was being ditched by . . . her little brother?!

CHAPTER

5

Tunnel Mayhem

I love Matt's shirt. Don't you just love his shirt?" Maeve whispered to Katani, admiring her tutor's trendy maroon and yellow striped tee.

"It's cool, I guess."

"And what about his eyes? Don't you just love Matt's eyes? I could look at them for hours." Maeve swooned quietly, as they trailed behind him through the crowd.

Katani frowned. "His eyes might be fascinating, but his jeans are kind of boring, don't you think? They're just straight-leg, double-pocket, non-pleated, stone-washed jeans. Pretty ordinary, really."

Maeve knew Katani was right, but she rushed to Matt's defense anyway. "I know, but on him they just look so . . . so . . . *uncommonly dreamy.*"

"I think you're the one who's dreaming," Charlotte said.

"Ha *ha*," Maeve replied. "You guys just don't know what it's like to be . . . oh never mind."

They didn't mind. Maeve's mega crushes changed at least

once a month; her friends had gotten used to it. They didn't doubt that Maeve was serious about her feelings . . . she just had, well, a lot of feelings.

Matt finally stopped in front of a booth that had a big, covered aquarium with a heat lamp shining on it like the sun. It was sort of a mini greenhouse, overflowing with lush, beautiful flowers in every color of the rainbow. Tiny purple buds and green leaves grew over the edge like a jungle curtain. Leading the exhibit was a tall girl with tortoise-shell glasses, freckles, and long brown hair worn half up in a messy bun. She had on a loose, flowing skirt, a silky light green shirt, a single beaded necklace, and a jean jacket.

Matt ran right up to the girl and swallowed her up in a big bear hug. "Everyone . . . I want you to meet my friend."

"Hi, girls. I'm Bailey."

Maeve gulped. Bailey? Why had she thought that Bailey was a boy? For a split second she wondered if maybe Bailey was *more than a friend*. But then she shook that thought away. Bailey was cute enough and everything, but she definitely didn't have Maeve's chic sense of style and glamour. No. No way would this girl be Matt's type.

"Bailey and I met last summer in our environmental biology class," Matt explained. "I took a class at MIT, and guess who was my lab partner?"

"I still can't believe I was stuck with this slacker, . . ." Bailey chided with a grin, fighting off Matt, who was trying to give her a noogie.

"Bailey, this is Maeve. The girl I was telling you about," said Matt.

Suddenly, Maeve felt like the sun was pouring down on

her and her alone. *The girl I was telling you about . . .* So Matt had been talking about her!

She held out her hand very properly and said, "Pleased to meet you."

"Your display is absolutely gorgeous," Katani interjected. "These colors are just . . . delicious." She pointed to a particularly vibrant pot of tangerine-colored blossoms. "You could not get fabric in *this* shade."

Bailey laughed and suddenly looked embarrassed. "These are my prizewinning peonies. I developed a custommade fertilizer from compost—I used leftover food from the school cafeteria. It's 100 percent organic."

Matt shook his head. "Bailey's Magic Plant Juice. I swear you should sell this stuff."

Bailey shrugged and giggled. "C'mon, Matt. You know I need to do more research . . . but someday, I hope."

Matt rolled his eyes. "Puh-lease. Even Professor Sutter asked her for her secret formula. This is actually a lot more intense than it looks. Bailey bred all these flowers from baby seedlings. She pollinated them in a lab."

"It took me three whole semesters to get it right," Bailey explained. "The lighting, the soil, the fertilizer. . . . But the good news is, now that I know what I'm doing, I think I might really be onto something."

Maeve gazed at the flowers, feeling slightly sorry for herself. Science came so naturally to some people, but it was so difficult for her. If only she had the talent to grow beautiful flowers from tiny seeds. She glanced over and noticed that Sam was busy reading Bailey's lab report. *Grr*, she thought. *He probably understands all this stuff.*

"Bailey, I'd love to stick around for a while, but we're actually on a bit of a scavenger hunt here. I'm trying to round up some kids. One of them has a real passion for the environment, so we thought maybe she'd be at your booth."

Bailey scratched her head. "Hmm . . . I've seen like a million kids today. What do they look like?"

Charlotte had a writer's eagle eye for details. "One is about up to here on me," she described, holding her hand up to her shoulder, "and was wearing a side ponytail and a soccer jersey with the number five. The other one is a little taller than I am, with long, shiny black hair, brown eyes. She was wearing this bird T-shirt. It said, um . . . what was that . . . oh, yeah: 'Polly want a little piece and quiet at the Boston Public Library.'"

Bailey laughed. "I think I'd certainly remember if I saw a T-shirt like that around. Sorry, though . . . no such luck."

"We have three of the girls now . . . ," Matt said, scanning the room.

"Three?" asked Bailey. "I'm only counting two."

"Shoot!" Matt exclaimed. "Don't tell me we lost another one!"

Sam, Maeve, and Charlotte looked around. "Katani?" Maeve called.

"Don't panic," Charlotte said soothingly. "Isn't that her over there in the yellow scarf?"

Maeve sprinted over to retrieve her. When they returned, Katani had a huge smile on her face. "Too bad they're packing up to go. I wish you could have checked out that booth, Char. If you thought the hydro-car was cool, you'd just flip over the waterwheel that spins and creates electricity. It reminds me of some stuff my dad showed me."

Matt used the bottom of his T-shirt to wipe sweat off his brow. "Keeping track of you kids is impossible. It's like herding cats," he said. "Now where in the world are Avery and Isabel?"

Maeve tried to ignore the fact that he just said "you kids." He must have meant everyone *but* her.

"Maybe their workshop ran a little late," Katani suggested.

"You're probably right," Matt agreed. "So I guess we'll just head back to the entrance and wait for them. I sure wish they'd hurry up, though. I promised to have you guys back in plenty of time for dinner, and if I'm going to show you the tunnels—"

Sam's hand suddenly shot into the air. "Ooh, ooh! Pick me! Pick me! I have an idea!"

Maeve groaned. "This isn't school, Sam. You *don't* have to raise your hand, you know."

"Let him talk, Maeve," instructed Matt.

Maeve felt stung and took a step back. Matt was totally treating her like a little kid!

Sam, like his big sis, cherished being the center of attention and explained as slowly as possible. "Wellllll . . . if we're just going to be waiting around for . . . we could see the tunnels now, and then meet them."

"But Avery really wants to check out the tunnels," Maeve protested. "We can't do it without her!"

"Actually, I think Sam has a good idea, Maeve," Matt replied. "If we don't go now, nobody's going to get to see the tunnels. We'll just meet them back at the entrance to the festival like we planned—*after* a little underground adventure!"

Matt playfully threw an arm around Sam's shoulders. "Forward, troops. To the tunnels we go. You coming, Bailey?"

She shook her head. "Can't. Someone's got to stay here and pack up the peonies."

The crew waved good-bye to Bailey and went off on their mission. Maeve walked slowly between Katani and Charlotte. She couldn't believe that Matt was paying more attention to her pesky little brother than her.

"What did you think of Bailey?" she whispered to Charlotte and Katani.

"Very nice," Charlotte remarked. "And very smart. Her fertilizer formula was pretty genius, really. Everybody wants to be green these days."

"I like her style, too," Katani noted.

Maeve gasped. "Seriously? Those clothes looked like they were from 1969! I swear, my mom has like, a thousand of those hippie skirts in boxes in our attic."

"Gosh, Maeve." Katani sighed. "Hippie chic is totally in vogue right now. The style's called *boho*. Short for bohemian."

"Boho," Maeve tried out the strange-sounding word. "More like *hobo*, if you ask me."

"Maeve!" Charlotte gasped. "Be nice!"

A wave of shame came over Maeve when she realized how catty she'd sounded. She didn't know what was wrong with her.

"C'mon guys!" Matt called. "We can get into the tunnels through this building right over here."

Maeve's stomach did a flip-flop. It suddenly occurred to her that she was going to be going underground. What if the tunnels were filled with spiderwebs? "Umm . . . if it's okay with you guys, maybe I should just stay right here, you know?"

Matt folded his arms. "Absolutely not, Maeve. From this point on we are sticking together. Understand?"

"Yes." She grabbed Charlotte's wrist as the girls descended down the stairs.

"Ouch! Maeve, you're hurting me!" Charlotte squeaked.

"Sorry," Maeve said, loosening her grip. "It's kind of hard to go down stairs in these boots—I don't want to fall!"

Katani had to laugh at that one. "Honey, you have got your arm on the wrong girl!" Klutzy Charlotte was the most disaster-prone girl in the seventh grade, but she didn't really mind. It was just something she learned to deal with. Sometimes she even cracked herself up with her crazy mishaps.

The insides of the tunnels were dimly lit, and the sounds of their footsteps echoed eerily on the ancient tile floor. "This would be the perfect setting for a scary movie," Charlotte admitted, squeezing Maeve's hand.

"Do you think this place might be a little bit haunted?" Maeve whispered. She heard creaking noises, and just when she thought it was safe, a little bug scuttled out in front of her feet. "Eeek!"

"Maeve, is that whining noise coming from you?" Katani accused.

"I can't help it," Maeve said in a breathless voice. "It's spooky down here. I feel like I might faint."

"You are such a drama queen, Maeve," Katani moaned. "It's just a tunnel. Hundreds of students must pass through here every day." Katani would not let a few butterflies in her stomach blow her cover of always being cool, confident, and composed.

"Chin up, Maeve!" hollered Matt. "I thought that Mix-Master-Curl was the toughest cookie on the block."

Maeve felt her mouth curl into a smile. He truly was a prince. *If I did happen to faint,* Maeve told herself, *surely Matt would catch me in his arms and carry me to safety.* Still, the creepy clangs and creaks wouldn't stop. "There is no way we're alone down here," she murmured.

All of a sudden, classical music started to play. Katani, Maeve, and even Sam jumped into the air and grabbed each other.

"Isn't that—" started Matt.

"Beethoven's Fifth!" Charlotte exclaimed as she shuffled through her purse. "It's my cell phone, you guys. My dad downloaded the ringtone online. I know, it's wicked dorky."

Maeve clutched her heart. "Char, you have got to tell your dad to choose something, like, ten times less creepy."

"I don't think Beethoven would like his music being called creepy." Charlotte laughed, flipping open her phone. "Hello? You're where? No! We're in the tunnels! No . . . don't come back. Stay right where you are." She flipped her phone closed. "That was Isabel, using Elena Maria's cell phone. She said she and Ave and Scott and Elena Maria are outside the entrance. They already checked out the tunnels—Avery was kind of disappointed. Isabel said they didn't get very creeped out."

"Well, I'm creeped out enough for all of us! Let's get out of here!" Maeve said. The group did an about-face and hurried towards the stairs that led into the building above.

"Can you believe it?" moaned Isabel, when everybody

was reunited. "These two went to the holography exhibit without me!"

Elena Maria and Scott giggled like they'd been up to serious mischief.

Matt just shrugged casually. "Well, good. See, I told you there'd be something for everyone here."

Avery rolled her eyes and whispered to the BSG, "I have a feeling that the only thing here my bro is interested in is Elena Maria!"

On the way home on the T, everyone was still totally jazzed about the festival. Their brains were definitely ticking over all the fascinating things they had learned and the cool people they'd met, but they weren't exactly as happy and light as usual. The festival had given them a lot to think about.

"Look at these photos," Isabel breathed to Maeve and Avery, who were sitting on either side of her. "How beautiful are these plants? But if people don't make more of an effort to control global warming, these algae will change. Then the fish that need them for food might not eat them. It's complicated . . . you know, it's a food web thing," Isabel said with a gulp.

"I know," Avery exclaimed. She was majorly into all issues environmental, and sometimes got pretty fired up about it. "People don't realize how small things can make a big difference to the health of our planet!"

"Like you, right, Ave?" Katani teased her short friend.

"You betcha!" Avery shot back with a grin.

Maeve squeezed Isabel's hand. "Maybe there's something you can do?" she said.

Isabel nodded. "I sure hope so. I'm going to e-mail Emily Sullivan when I get home."

"It's too bad that the AAJH science fair can't be all about the environment," Avery lamented.

Charlotte stopped chatting with Sam in midsentence and whipped around. "Well, why can't it?"

Avery shrugged. "I dunno. I just thought it was supposed to be whatever science thing you wanted to learn about . . . you know?"

Matt smiled. "Well, according to Al Gore, the environment isn't just going to be *an* issue for the future of our Earth . . . it's already *the* issue."

"Oo! Oo! Oo!" Avery hooted excitedly, practically bouncing out of her seat. "This could work! We should totally make the AAJH science fair all about saving the planet!"

"If you guys truly feel passionate about environmental issues, that would be a very cool idea," Matt agreed.

"You really think?" asked Maeve.

Matt shrugged. "Hey. Why not? Didn't I tell you Mix-Master-Curl could do anything? Especially with your BSG posse around."

Maeve felt herself glowing as she watched the city of Cambridge, next door to Boston and Brookline, rush by her window. All in all, she thought, it had been one fabulous day . . . even the science was cool.

CHAPTER

6

A Shocking Surprise

Maeve couldn't believe how tired she was when she returned home from the Festival. *Phew! College is seriously a ton of work*, she thought. *Not just all the learning and everything, but running around all over that big, beautiful campus. And on top of all of that, I'm supposed to make sure my hair doesn't get frizzy! In five years or something, am I really going to be cut out for college? It's not like I'm Betsy Fitzgerald.* Maeve sighed. Betsy was AAJH's superstar student, who was dedicated to growing her college résumé at every opportunity.

As Maeve made her way up the stairs of the apartment, she caught a glimpse of herself in the mirror. She was pleased to find that each strand of her straight-for-the-day hairdo was absolutely perfect. *Huh. Maybe I am cut out for this after all.* Maeve flashed herself a gloriously glam smile, and began daydreaming about what her life would be like when she was old enough to be a real college student.

First of all, she was definitely going to have a boyfriend as cute as Matt. Maybe they would work on a science fair project like Bailey's together . . . someday. The thought of growing plants from tiny seedlings, making sure that they were properly cared for and turning out beautiful pink flowers for everyone to enjoy, made Maeve feel all glowy inside.

When Maeve arrived at her room, she flung open the door, and was totally ready to throw herself on her big, pink, plushy bed, when she noticed something blocking her dramatic moment: a large brown shopping bag. This was very strange, Maeve thought. It wasn't anywhere near her birthday or anything.

Tied on the handle of the bag with a pink ribbon was a small card with a note. Maeve opened the card and slowly read the words. "Maeve, let me know if this fits. My girl is growing up!!! XOXO ~ Love Mom."

Maeve's stomach did a tiny flip-flop as she wondered what might be lying beneath the light pink tissue paper. It was certainly something sophisticated—there was no doubt about that! Maeve hoped it would be the cute jean skirt that she'd been eyeing in the window of Think Pink—her favorite local boutique and pink stuff headquarters. Every day when she drove by Think Pink with her mom, she oohed and aahed over that lovely sequined pink denim number. Maybe her mom had finally picked up on her not-so-subtle hints.

Maeve never had much patience for suspense. It took her all of two seconds to pull out the tissue paper, shake it, and rip it up into shreds, revealing a small piece of white fabric. But it definitely took Maeve less than half a second to realize exactly what that little piece of white fabric *was*.

A bra.

A training bra?

A really, really, *really*, totally not cute training bra.

Maeve used her thumb and forefinger to pick up the garment, slowly—very slowly—and hold it up an arm's length away to give it an inspection. She wanted a bra, but Maeve had always imagined that her very *first* bra would be . . . well . . . something not quite so *blah*. Something silky maybe, with lace, and teeny tiny rosebuds. But this, this, *thing* . . . Ugh.

As Maeve put on her coziest pajamas, she knew there was no getting around it—sooner or later she was going to have to talk to her mom about this little "present." She just didn't realize how soon until she heard a quiet knock on her door. "Yoo-hoo, honey. It's me. Your mother. Can I come in?"

"Sure."

Ms. Kaplan hesitantly creaked open the door, crept in slowly, and took a seat next to Maeve on her bed. She was moving so cautiously, Maeve wondered if her mom thought her bed was going to explode or something. "Soooo . . . tell me. Did you have a good time at the science festival today?"

Maeve shrugged. "It was okay, I guess. Definitely cooler than I thought it would be."

"Really? How so?"

Maeve looked dreamily out the window, remembering how dashing Matt had been when he'd led the group through the creepy tunnel. "Oh, I dunno. They had some booths with science stuff that was really awesome. I can't believe how much those MIT kids know about the environment. This girl Bailey was growing the most awesome plants with her special organic fertilizer. And Sally Ride, the first American woman astronaut, was there. And of course Matt was like, the awesomest tour guide *ever*. He makes me feel like a real grown-up, you know?"

Maeve's mother burst into a smile of relief. "I'm so glad you feel that way, Maeve. In fact, that is exactly what I was hoping to talk to you about tonight."

"Matt making me feel like a grown-up?"

"No," Ms. Kaplan began, "I was going to talk to you about you *becoming* a grown-up. Did you see the surprise I left on your bed for you?"

"Oh . . . that." Maeve felt herself blush.

"Yes, *that*." Maeve noticed that her mom looked pretty uncomfortable too. "So . . . did you like it? Did you try it on?"

"Actually . . ."

"Well?"

Maeve saw how hopeful and sweet her mom's face looked. Now she didn't feel so much embarrassed—she just didn't want to hurt her mother's feelings by telling her that the bra she'd bought was far from the kind of bra that Maeve herself would ever want. So she decided to go with a little phrase that Katani had taught her when they were shopping together. Katani explained that this was what she said to Kelley when she didn't like what Kelley picked out. Maeve opened up her mouth, took a deep breath, and went for it. "To be honest, I wasn't *crazy* about it."

"Not crazy about it?" Ms. Kaplan got up and fetched the bra from the bag. She held it up and inspected it from every angle. Maeve felt her humiliation creeping right back immediately. "Not crazy about it?" she repeated. She seemed confused. "I don't get it, Maeve. It's only a training bra, after all.

It's not supposed to be like those ridiculous things on those, those, you know, Dream commercials."

Maeve shook her head. How was it possible for her mother to be so tragically out of touch with all things that were cool?

"I thought that the bra I picked out would be just perfect for you. The lady at the department store said it would fit most girls your age because the material was so stretchy."

"And uncomfortable," Maeve informed her. "I feel itchy just *looking* at it."

Ms. Kaplan tapped her chin. "But I just thought . . . mmm. When I was your age I was way too embarrassed to ask my mom about getting a bra. She just sort of figured out when that time had come and left one on my bed like I did for you. Not cool, huh?" Her Mom looked over at Maeve with a half smile.

"Um, Mom," Maeve began, taking a deep breath. "It's really nice that you did this for me. I mean, it's really, really sweet. But the thing is, when I imagined what my first bra would be like, I totally was thinking something way cuter— no offense, Mom."

Ms. Kaplan shook her head, smiling. "You have always had a very strong sense of style, Maeve. So what did you have in mind, hon?"

"I dunno, like maybe something with a little more . . . lace . . . and like, little pearls? Ooh, and also, teeny tiny rose-buds, you know? Maybe it could even be pink. You know, my signature color!" Maeve suggested. When she saw her mother looking like she was about to laugh, Maeve figured she'd better hurry up and get the point across. "I mean, if I absolutely must wear a bra, it should be just as cute as the clothes I want to wear over it . . . don't you think?"

Her mother nodded, patiently folded up the training bra, and placed it back in the shopping bag. "Well, I appreciate your honesty, sweetie. How about if you and I take a trip to the mall together on Monday to pick out a few together?"

Maeve smiled. "Really? Ones that I like?"

Ms. Kaplan squinted an eye. "Ones that we *agree on*."

Maeve jumped up and hugged her mom. "Thank you, thank you, thank you!" she cried.

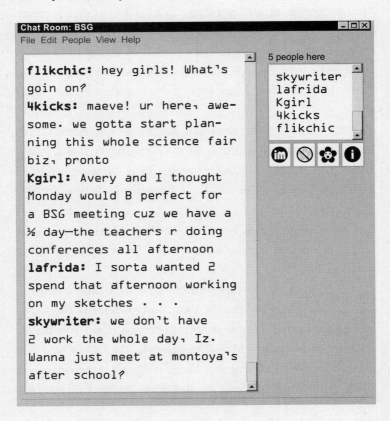

Chat Room: BSG

File Edit People View Help

flikchic: hey girls! What's goin on?

4kicks: maeve! ur here, awesome. we gotta start planning this whole science fair biz, pronto

Kgirl: Avery and I thought Monday would B perfect for a BSG meeting cuz we have a ½ day—the teachers r doing conferences all afternoon

lafrida: I sorta wanted 2 spend that afternoon working on my sketches . . .

skywriter: we don't have 2 work the whole day, Iz. Wanna just meet at montoya's after school?

5 people here

skywriter
lafrida
Kgirl
4kicks
flikchic

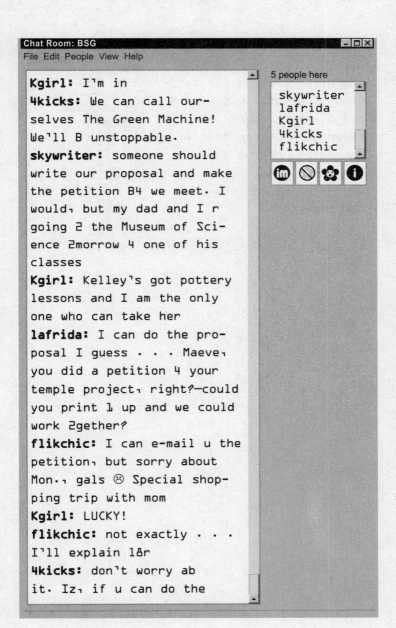

Kgirl: I'm in

4kicks: We can call ourselves The Green Machine!
We'll B unstoppable.

skywriter: someone should
write our proposal and make
the petition B4 we meet. I
would, but my dad and I r
going 2 the Museum of Science 2morrow 4 one of his
classes

Kgirl: Kelley's got pottery
lessons and I am the only
one who can take her

lafrida: I can do the proposal I guess . . . Maeve,
you did a petition 4 your
temple project, right?—could
you print 1 up and we could
work 2gether?

flikchic: I can e-mail u the
petition, but sorry about
Mon., gals ☹ Special shopping trip with mom

Kgirl: LUCKY!

flikchic: not exactly . . .
I'll explain l8r

4kicks: don't worry ab
it. Iz, if u can do the

5 people here

skywriter
lafrida
Kgirl
4kicks
flikchic

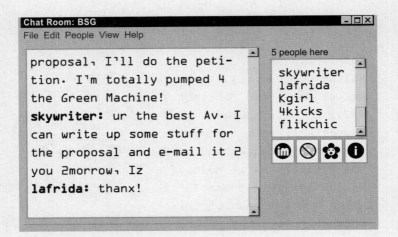

proposal, I'll do the petition. I'm totally pumped 4
the Green Machine!
skywriter: ur the best Av. I
can write up some stuff for
the proposal and e-mail it 2
you 2morrow, Iz
lafrida: thanx!

CHAPTER

7

Mission: Petition

"M orning, Ms. R!" Maeve called out as she marched into Ms. Rodriguez's homeroom. The BSG were huddled around their desks enjoying the precious five minutes before class started. Sometimes, Ms. R would sit at her desk, sip her coffee, and read the paper, giving her class a chance to unwind so they could focus on the lesson of the day. Happily, this was one of those days. And no one appreciated this mini social time more than Maeve Kaplan-Taylor, who was strutting over to her girlfriends as if the front of the classroom were her own personal catwalk.

"You guys like my outfit?" Maeve asked. "I decided to go green for the big Green Machine kickoff. What do you think?" Maeve spun around to show off her khaki pleated skirt and an asparagus-colored cotton sweater. She had turned in her signature pink wardrobe for earth tones and was feeling especially proud of herself.

"You know, girl, I will say, this is a refreshing fashion choice," noted clothing-conscious Katani, who often thought that Maeve's pink on pink on pink choices bordered on a little tacky. "But supporting earth colors isn't exactly the same thing as supporting the Earth."

Maeve threw her backpack down on a desk. "Well, obviously! But dressing the part to get into the spirit of things never hurt anyone! Why do you think people wear costumes on Halloween? Duh."

Charlotte opened her mouth to comment on the historical significance of Halloween costumes but then decided not to bother. Maeve, in her own weird way, did have a point.

"Now, Avery," Katani began, whipping out a sunshine yellow pad of paper. "Did you bring the petition?"

"Roger that, Kgirl!" Avery dove into her bag and riffled through her sloppily shoved-in folders and packets. Katani couldn't imagine keeping her stuff so messy and cringed as Avery finally produced a crinkled sheet of paper. "Check it out, my fellow environmental warriors," she announced proudly. "The Green Machine Official Mission to Save the Planet Earth. On recycled paper, of course. I even put on this clip art picture of the planet. Pretty cool, huh, Iz?" Avery glanced at Isabel for her artistic approval.

"Totally!" Isabel said with a sweet smile as she fished something out of her bag. "Here is the proposal I did. Well, Charlotte wrote it, and I designed it. What do you think?"

Like every project Isabel took on, her proposal looked flashy and fabulous. It was no secret to everyone at AAJH that Isabel was a gifted artist. The BSG gave one another happy nods that their talented friend had, once again, come up with a complete success. Best of all, Isabel had decorated the paper so fantastically, it would be impossible for people who saw it not to want to read on. On the top of the page was one of Isabel's signature bird cartoons. Charlotte thought this one was particularly on target.

Charlotte had described the girls' mission to focus their science fair projects on ways in which they could improve the environment, with recycling, energy conservation and alternative energy, green and natural building, and carbon emissions control . . . all the neat stuff they had learned about at the festival.

Katani scribbled on her pad and said very matter-of-factly, "Petition . . . check. Proposal . . . check."

"Immature hairstyles . . . check!" sang a voice from behind the BSG. The girls didn't have to turn around to know it was Anna with her sidekick Joline by her side. "What's the big meeting about, girls?" Anna snickered sarcastically, leaning over Katani's shoulder. "Something really important, I bet!"

Even though Charlotte truly didn't care one bit about what Anna or Joline thought, when those Queens of Mean treated her and her friends so nastily, she always felt nervous and sick to her stomach. Maybe it was the leftover effects of her being a new kid so many times—she was used to feeling like the odd girl out. But she admired how poised Katani was when it came to the terrible twosome.

Katani didn't blink or even give Anna the satisfaction of turning around. "Nothing, Anna. The meeting is about nothing, so it's none of your business."

"Oh, well that's where you're wrong. See . . . everything at Abigail Adams Junior High is *my business*. I am one of the two seriously gifted columnists for the Sentinel gossip column after all. I make a point of knowing absolutely everything."

Joline nodded as she quickly combed her fingers through her long, stick-straight brown hair. Joline never stopped playing with her hair. Maeve wrinkled her nose and wondered if maybe that was some kind of nervous tic.

"Come on, seriously, Katani. What are you guys working on? It better not be some kind of practical joke . . . cause that's against the AAJH rules, you know," Anna smugly informed them.

"And we'll tell Ms. R. Don't think we won't," added Joline.

Avery stood straight up, stepped right in front of Anna, and looked her in the eye, which wasn't easy, as Avery's head barely reached Anna's shoulder. "Listen up, blondie. It just so happens that we are starting a petition to save our planet. Earth as we know and love it is changing big-time. Like melting glaciers that can raise sea levels—imagine certain peoples' beach houses, like Kiki Underwood's for example, sliding into the ocean!"

Avery was speaking so loudly that now all of Ms. Rodriguez's class had become quiet to hear what she had to say. Ms. R glanced up from her paper calmly. She knew that when Avery Madden had something to say, it was usually interesting. She nodded at Avery to continue.

Realizing that she had gained the spotlight, Avery decided to take it a step further, and jumped up on her chair so for once she was the tallest in the room. "Imagine a billion people on our planet don't even have clean water! Imagine living with water that's contaminated by garbage or even sewage."

"Ew, gross!" Joline squealed.

"Gross is right!" Avery cried, throwing her fist in the air.

"That is why we, the Green Machine, are asking you, fellow classmates, to sign our petition and agree to focus your science fair projects on our planet, Mother Earth. One seventh-grader can't save the whole giant planet by herself, but if we all get inspired and everybody does something—even a little thing—together we can make a difference!"

Charlotte and Isabel glanced at each other, remembering the time Avery ran for class president. Even though she had lost to Henry Yurt, she'd spearheaded a fabulous campaign, and it was clear that a career in getting people motivated was definitely in Avery Madden's future.

"So if you want to join our cause to save the one and only planet we call our home, then step right up and sign the dotted line. Actually, it's more like a solid line, now that I look at it, but whatever! It's a line!" Avery shook the wrinkled paper high above her head like she was holding the Declaration of Independence.

Anna rolled her eyes at Joline and whispered, "How pathetically uncool."

"But of course," Katani intervened in a soft voice, "we don't want just anybody signing the petition."

Avery looked outraged and jumped down from her chair. "Katani, are you crazy? That's exactly what we—*ouch*!" She felt someone step on her toe and realized that it was Katani.

"We're really just looking for smart and talented people who *actually care* about making a difference." Katani emphasized the words "actually care" as she glanced at the Queens of Mean. "We don't want people signing up just to look cool and be part of the most awesome science fair this school has ever had. Nope, we only want people who are truly passionate about saving the environment." Katani took the petition and held it close to her chest. "No Green Machine wannabes. Period."

Joline looked at Anna, panic-stricken. "I care about the environment! Honestly, I do! My family and I were the ones who started my neighborhood's own farmer's market. Eat local!"

Anna glared at Joline. "You are such a copycat! That was totally my idea! I told you about that two months ago!"

Joline frowned. "Oh yeah? Then why did I start our farmer's market *three* months ago?"

"Liar! Hey, Katani, can you pass me that petition? I am very, very concerned about saving the environment. Way more concerned than Joline."

"Wait, Katani! Pass me the Green Machine petition! I'm the concerned one!" The BSG watched, astounded, as Anna and Joline battled to be the first person to sign the Green Machine petition.

Katani turned to the BSG with a satisfied smile. Her plan had worked! Tell the Queens of Mean that they weren't wanted, and they just *had* to be there. And if the Queens of Mean had to be there, so did everybody else. In about five seconds, everyone in Ms. Rodriguez's homeroom was lined up behind Anna and Joline to sign the petition—including Ms. R!

By the time the final bell rang that day—sooner than usual because it was a half day—Avery had in her hand six and a half sheets of signatures. Maeve had nearly fainted when the Crow, her math teacher and the one faculty member she liked to avoid, stopped her after math to sign his name too! "It's about time we put our hearts and minds into such a worthy project," he declared, signing "Maxwell J. Sherman" on Maeve's copy of the petition with a flourish.

"And check this out," started Katani, as a flood of kids ran right past them, shouting, whistling, and ready to take advantage of half a day of freedom. "My grandma even promised to bring it up at the faculty meeting today. She thinks it's high time for a green science fair, and she admires our initiative." Katani's grandmother, Mrs. Fields, also happened to be the principal of AAJH. She was very kind to the BSG, but also very fair. When she had her principal hat on, Mrs. Fields did not play favorites. That was why a compliment from her really meant a lot.

"So is the next stop Montoya's Bakery for some more Green Machine planning?" Charlotte asked.

"What?" Isabel cupped her ear. "I can't hear you over all the screaming." The girls looked around at the hallway full of smiling faces and loud, happy voices.

"Hey, Char! Catch!" shouted Nick Montoya, throwing Charlotte a softball as he passed. Charlotte, startled, missed the ball, which landed by her feet. She spun around to find it, and as she did, stepped on the ball. Her feet got all tangled up under her and she began swinging her arms like a windmill to keep from falling. It was a typical Charlotte klutz-o-rama moment—one for her journal. Nick, in a very gentlemanly way, reached out his hand to steady Charlotte as her face turned as red as a plum tomato.

"We're playing ball at the field," Nick informed the BSG, ignoring Charlotte's acute embarrassment. "You coming?"

Since Charlotte's favorite part of Montoya's bakery wasn't

going to be at the bakery that afternoon, she was more than happy to change plans. "I'll go," she said softly.

"Sounds good to me!" Isabel piped.

"Sounds like *procrastination* to me," Maeve announced, sternly folding her arms. In her head she was playing the role of bookish, super-serious student. A sudden nervous feeling in the pit of her stomach had her intent on putting off the bra shopping trip, and planning for a green science fair seemed like an excuse her mom might go for. Playing ball, not so much.

The BSG turned to Maeve with faces of utter shock. "Excuuuse me?" Avery gasped. "I'm sorry, is there some sort of strange homework spirit which has momentarily taken possession of Maeve? 'Cause last time I checked, MK-T was the procrastination *queen*."

"I just think that if we get behind schedule now, then we'll never finish our projects on time, and then you know what will suffer? The Earth," Maeve argued.

The girls looked as if they'd spotted a UFO. "Um, Maeve, I don't think a few extra hours of fun will be the end of our projects . . . and it definitely won't be the end of the Earth," Katani said, her mouth curling into the beginning of a smile. "I vote . . . fun?"

"WHOOOO HOOOOO!" Avery cheered, jumping up and down. "Let's plaaaaay ball!"

Maeve had no choice. She watched, for the second time that week, as the BSG skipped away and she was left alone to trudge home. Usually shopping was an activity Maeve would be very much excited about. But—for one very good reason that began with a "B"—she was soooo not her usual self today!

Goldi-Maeve and the Three Bras

"Mom, I think these pink ones are totally me." Maeve was holding up a pair of pink fake-sheepskin boots on display in the large department store's shoe section.

"Come on, Maeve. We don't have time to dawdle. Your brother gets out of Tae Kwon Do in an hour." Ms. Kaplan anxiously scanned the store and marched over to a lady wearing a nametag and holding a bottle of perfume. "Excuse me, ma'am. Where is the underwear department?"

"The *lingerie* department," the snooty sales girl said, correcting her mother, "is up the escalator and to the left. Would you care for a spritz of Hello? It's the new fragrance by Lucy C."

"Definitely not," Ms. Kaplan replied, signaling for Maeve to follow her.

"There's a free gift . . . ," the girl hollered behind them.

"Ooh, free gift, Mom! I just *love* free gifts. Can't we just—"

"Don't be fooled, honey. There's no such thing as a free gift," the ever-practical Ms. Kaplan informed her daughter. "And besides, that sales girl was a little rude."

"But if you bought that perfume and gave the gift to me, then it's free . . . for me. See? I'm a genius," Maeve reasoned with a giggle as she followed her mother up the escalator into the lingerie department.

In front of Maeve stretched a silky white wonderland. Two mannequins wearing beautiful lacy night gowns and curly blonde wigs welcomed the shoppers to the lingerie department.

"Wow." Maeve breathed. "Toto, we are sooooo not in Kansas anymore." Maeve gulped. She knew that bras came in different styles, but she had no idea there were quite so many. On past shopping trips she'd never paid much attention. Now, the aisles of bras seemed to go on forever. They had a bra for every color of the rainbow! Maeve ran right over to a rack of bras in pomegranate pink.

"I found it, Mom," Maeve called. "This is the one."

Ms. Kaplan shook her head. "No way, kiddo."

"But Moooom . . ."

"Look, Maeve. I know you love pink. But that is not appropriate."

Maeve opened her mouth to protest, but then she realized her mother was probably right.

"Look. I'm going to go ask a saleslady what bras would be best for someone who's still developing."

"Mom!" Maeve groaned. She hated that word—developing. She was a person, not a photograph.

"Why don't you take a look around and try—I mean it, Maeve—try to find something reasonable," Ms. Kaplan suggested. As she walked away, Maeve heard her mother sigh. "My little girl is growing up!"

As much as Maeve appreciated her mother's wisdom, she was relieved to have a little time alone to shop. Her mother's idea of reasonable and her idea of reasonable were very different things. As she was deciding which way to wander first, she suddenly heard a melodious voice behind her.

"Oh, it's no problem," the woman said smoothly. "I can take that for you, miss." As Maeve turned around, she immediately noticed the woman's outfit. Hair in a sleek French twist, shiny silk blouse paired with a black pencil skirt, peep-toe black pumps, and matching gold earrings and long necklace.

She looked the way movie stars did when they lunched with producers. Maeve was impressed.

She walked over as the woman gracefully handed a bag to the customer, then turned her attention to Maeve and smiled. "I'm Marlena. Let me guess. You're looking for a pretty bra, am I right?"

"Yes, that's exactly right!" Maeve squeaked, feeling a little overwhelmed but also super excited. This Marlena woman looked like she knew what she was talking about when it came to lingerie.

"And practical," Ms. Kaplan added, walking over.

"Yes, of course," Marlena purred. "Here we are." She directed Maeve and her mother to a rack full of bras covered in lace and ribbons. Maeve thought that, hanging all together like that, they looked like one big spiderweb. "The perfect bra for a high-fashion young lady like you. Chic, sophisticated, glamorous lace for miles . . ."

Maeve's mother looked shocked. "No. No. No. We're looking for something less . . . um . . . sophisticated. I just don't think that's going to work," Ms. Kaplan said. "Don't you have anything . . . you know . . . white? Something a little more conservative?"

"White!" Marlena exclaimed. "I think my coworker, Connie, can help you with a sports bra, if you like." She spun around and charged after a lady carrying a leopard-print bag the size of a suitcase.

"It doesn't have to be white!" Maeve called after her, but Marlena was gone. Maeve pouted. "I sort of liked that last one . . ."

Ms. Kaplan gave her a look. "Seriously, Maeve. You knew

that was as absurd as I did—that bra might as well have been made of plastic wrap!" Maeve looked at her mom and they burst out laughing together.

Suddenly, a monotone voice sounded behind them. "May I help you?" The woman tapped her name tag. "So. You want something white and sporty?"

Maeve worked up her courage and spoke. "Well, it doesn't have to be white. I think pink would be nice, too . . ."

Connie, the expert on sports bras, turned and gestured for them to follow her. "This way, ladies."

Maeve and her mother practically ran after Connie, who was moving very quickly down the aisles. Finally, she stopped beside a rack full of white sports bras . . . very plain white sports bras.

Maeve cringed and looked up to see her mother making the exact same face. *Wow,* thought Maeve. *If these bras are too ugly for my mom, they must be seriously bad!*

"It looks better on," Connie offered tonelessly.

"Um . . . thanks, Connie," Ms. Kaplan said politely. "But I think we'll take it from here and just look around."

Connie shrugged and said, "I'll be over there," and wandered off toward the register.

"Mom, I think that lady needs a personality adjustment!" Maeve whispered, watching Connie walk away.

"Maeve!" her mother scolded. Then she admitted, "She did seem a bit . . . subdued."

Maeve sighed and crossed her arms over her chest. She was feeling frustrated and disappointed. "Maybe we should just go, Mom. I don't think we're going to find anything here."

"Oh, let's not give up just yet."

"But I feel like Goldilocks, Mom! Those first bras were way too fancy . . . then that one Connie showed us was just . . . ugh." She shivered a little, thinking about the extreme ugliness of that bra. "Will I ever find one that's just right?"

Ms. Kaplan smiled at her dramatic daughter. "I think you will, Maeve. There's bound to be something perfect among these hundreds," she said as she gestured at the rows of bras.

Maeve stared at the sea of "lingerie" around her and suddenly felt too worn down to shop, which was bad . . . especially for Maeve. Disappointed, she followed her mother around the store like a sad puppy as Ms. Kaplan haphazardly pulled off anything that looked like it could possibly fit her daughter. "Here," Ms. Kaplan said, thrusting a pile of fabric at Maeve. "Try these on to start, and I'll meet you in the dressing room."

Maeve nodded wordlessly and shuffled into the ladies room, feeling Connie's weird eyes upon her as she passed. *Awkward!* Maeve thought with a shudder.

She slipped into a dressing room and got to work. Unfortunately, none of the bras was at all acceptable on Maeve's cute-o-meter. They weren't as bad as Connie's pick, but they were all just so *ordinary*. She slumped down on the stool in the dressing room in defeat, kicking the pile of bras on the floor as she swung her legs back and forth.

Suddenly she heard a familiar voice coming from the changing room beside her. "He's so cute, and so nice . . . but I just can't figure out if he likes me or not!"

Maeve gasped. It was Elena Maria.

"Are you kidding me? Of course he likes you! Whenever

you walk by he turns bright red and can barely even speak. I think it's adorable," replied another girl.

"Well, even if he did like me, it's not like there's anything I can do about it . . . Jimmy would flip."

Maeve, who did not want to be caught listening, quickly gathered up her clothes and tried to run back out of the changing room unseen. Unfortunately, this just didn't seem to be a lucky day for her.

"Maeve! Wh-what are you doing here!" Elena Maria cried.

Busted! Maeve slowly turned around to meet Elena Maria's eyes. She recognized the girl with her as one of Elena Maria's best friends, Cammy Dooley. Cammy was known as a little bit of a gossip anyway, which made Maeve feel not quite as bad for accidentally listening in.

Maeve didn't know what was worse—being caught with an armful of bras, or being caught listening to her best friend's older sister's private conversation. "I was just. You know. Shopping . . ." Her cheeks felt very warm.

Elena Maria looked around, and Maeve noticed that her cheeks were burning too. "Did you, um, hear what we were talking about?"

"Well, duh, Elena! She was right there . . . ," Cammy pointed out.

"Maeve . . ." A slow smile crept into the corner of Elena Maria's mouth. "Are you . . . *bra shopping*?"

There was no denying the mountain of bras in Maeve's arms. "Sorta, kinda, yeah," Maeve admitted. "This is actually my first time," she added shyly.

"No way! How's it going?" asked Elena Maria.

Maeve shook her head. "Not so good. My mom's

somewhere around here, trying to help, I guess. But, Elena, ugh, our taste is just so not the same!"

Elena Maria nodded. "It was the same with my mom. But all the preteen bras are usually tucked away towards the back and some are mixed in with some of the sports bras. No one tells the mothers that. Now, check these out!" Elena Maria and Cammy led the way through several aisles to a rack of bras near the back, which Maeve deemed absolutely perfect.

Maeve selected some bras in a few different sizes and tried them on in a flash. She ran out of the dressing room with a huge smile pasted to her face. "Miracle of miracles!" Maeve exclaimed, quoting a song from *Fiddler on the Roof*— one of her absolute favorite musicals. "I found some that fit and are super cute! And they're on sale too. Buy one get one free. My mom is going to be soooo happy."

Elena Maria offered Maeve a good-natured smile. "Well, I'm happy to help. Will you just promise me one thing?"

"Sure," Maeve replied. "Anything."

"Um, just don't mention to the BSG what you heard us talking about in the dressing room . . . I'd be really embarrassed . . ."

Maeve put her hand over her heart. "Absolutely. You have my word. And . . . um . . . can you keep it private about seeing me here, either? I haven't exactly told them about . . . you know . . . getting a bra, yet."

Elena Maria extended her pinky for a good, old-fashioned pinky swear. The girls locked fingers and Elena Maria assured her, "Don't worry for an instant, Maeve. Your secret's safe with me!"

As Maeve waved good-bye to the two older girls, she

couldn't help envying Isabel. How lucky she was to have such a cool, knowledgeable older sister.

Ms. Kaplan and Maeve were very quiet as they left the department store with their bag. Maeve was thrilled that her mother insisted on a new nightgown, too—what an unexpected treat!

"Now that wasn't too painful, right, sweetie?" asked Ms. Kaplan as they pulled out of the mall parking lot.

"Not even a little bit," Maeve agreed. "Thank you for everything, Mom. You're the best." Maeve gave her mother's hand a squeeze, but Ms. Kaplan didn't say anything back. Instead she turned on the radio and started making a little squeaking noise as the music blared over the speakers. It wasn't until Maeve noticed that her mom was dabbing her eyes with the wrist of her sweater that Maeve realized her mother was crying!

"Mom . . ." Maeve began. "Are you okay?"

Ms. Kaplan sniffled. "I'm fine, sweetie. But I feel like just yesterday you were throwing spaghetti noodles at me and learning how to walk."

Maeve smiled. "If it helps, I can still throw spaghetti noodles at you . . ."

Ms. Kaplan snorted out a laugh as the music shifted to the Beatles. It was one of Maeve's favorites: "Ob-la-di, Ob-la-da." Maeve wondered why she had never noticed the chorus before, which went "Ob-la-di, Ob-la-da, life goes on . . ."

Life does *go on*, Maeve thought. *I really* am *growing up*. She and her mother sang the song at the top of their lungs all the way home. Maeve had to admit—it had turned out to be a perfectly wonderful day.

CHAPTER

8

The Green Machine

W hen Maeve walked into school the next day, she couldn't help feeling a little nervous about her secret. She wondered if people could tell that underneath her crisp white blouse and pink plaid skirt she was wearing a bra for the first time ever! What in the world would the BSG say if they only knew? But she quickly learned that the BSG had things on their minds besides the great MK-T's underwear status.

"Did you hear the news? Mrs. Fields just called an assembly in the gym!" Avery announced, grabbing Maeve by the elbow.

"An assembly! Is everything all right?" Maeve asked, suddenly feeling a bit of panic.

"Well, we aren't supposed to know anything." Charlotte grinned.

"You can blame me for spilling the beans," Katani admitted. "Everything is fine. Just fine. But the assembly's about the science fair."

Maeve jumped up and down and clapped excitedly. "No way! Does that mean what I think it means?" she cried, following the swarm of students into the auditorium. Inside, the big room had been decorated to look sort of like a tropical rain forest—complete with five huge papier-mâché birds. "Balloons and cupcakes! This place looks incredible!" Maeve gushed, recognizing one of her friends' handiwork immediately. "Did you have something to do with this, Missy?" Maeve asked, jokingly wagging her finger at Isabel.

Isabel giggled. "Guilty as charged. It would have been better too . . . but the whole thing was kind of last minute. A bunch of kids helped."

"Including me," proudly added Katani. Kgirl and Isabel's creative forces combined were truly unstoppable.

Once the students were settled in their seats, Mrs. Fields wasted no time. "The faculty at Abigail Adams Junior High is pleased to announce that this year, for the first time ever, we are hosting a science fair that is one hundred percent environmentally oriented!"

The BSG looked around at the enthusiastic faces around them and felt a wash of excitement pass over them as the whole auditorium erupted in applause.

"Thanks to the efforts of everyone who signed a petition, put together by a motivated group of students known as . . ." Mrs. Fields cleared her throat and said in a loud, clear voice, *"The Green Machine!"*

The girls made a link with their hands and gave one another a tight squeeze. Charlotte pondered how nice it was that her friends had reached a point where they could totally communicate everything they were feeling without even using words. That was truly something special, and one of the many things she loved about being BFFs with the BSG.

"I am also happy to tell you all that anyone—even teachers—who would like to join the Green Machine movement is welcome to sign up. We have given information sheets—printed on recycled paper, of course—to every homeroom teacher," said Mrs. Fields. The room filled with confused whispers, and Mrs. Fields quickly tapped the microphone to clarify. "Allow me to explain. All students must put together a science fair project which has some sort of environmental theme. *But*—if you would like to go above and beyond, that is, help organize and spearhead the science fair, the Green Machine will gladly be taking on more members, which will count as an after school activity . . . as well as extra credit."

Now the whispering got even louder. The BSG heard some of their fellow classmates from Ms. R's room getting especially excited. "Extra credit? For doing something I already love?" Betsy Fitzgerald, the resident class overachiever, was murmuring to Nick Montoya. "Can you imagine how fabulous this will look on my résumé?"

Nick laughed, but nodded in agreement. "I love doing stuff outside anyway, and I mean, I could totally use the extra credit. This Green Machine thing rocks!" he added, quickly glancing at Charlotte.

Maeve raised her eyebrows at Charlotte, who immediately looked down with rosy cheeks. Even though Maeve knew Nick Montoya loved being outside playing sports, she also knew he would do just about anything to get closer to Charlotte Ramsey.

"Anyone who would like to join the Green Machine is

invited on the stage for a very special cheer," Mrs. Fields called.

Avery jumped up with a huge grin, pulled Katani to her feet, and started dragging her toward the stage without looking back. Katani gave her friends a desperate glance. "Will you guys come up with us? Avery and I sort of already promised my grandma . . ."

There was probably a time when Charlotte would have been way too bashful to get up on stage and do anything, especially with her track record for humiliating moments. But as the rest of the BSG rose from their seats, she was surprised that she didn't even have to think twice about the whole thing. In fact, other groups of kids were getting up too . . . including Anna and Joline.

As everyone lined up on stage, a drumming noise began to grow louder and louder from the outside hallway. Suddenly, the doors burst open. Maeve shrieked and covered her mouth as the junior high school football team marched in . . . all wearing matching T-shirts with pictures of green algae on them.

Once again, Maeve turned towards Isabel, who looked down shyly. "What can I say? I had a little extra time on my hands this weekend to come up with a design. I was totally inspired by Emily Sullivan's algae. And it's printed with soy ink!"

Katani beamed. "I had the T-shirts made at this great little shop I know. Think they're cotton? Nope—bamboo! Really. Bamboo is amazing. It grows really fast, without pesticides or chemicals, plus it's a hundred percent biodegradable. As soon as I told the people at the shop that it was for our school science fair, they donated as many as we needed!" There was no doubt about it—Kgirl was a fashion enterprising genius.

The AAJH football team was acting really goofy and obviously having tons of fun as they conga-ed down the center of the auditorium to a marine style rhythm, shouting, "Embrace the Green, embrace the Green Machine!" It wasn't long before the entire room had joined in the catchy chant. It was official: Abigail Adams had whole-heartedly embraced the Green! And at the root of it all was the BSG. The girls felt like in two seconds flat they'd nearly be bursting with pride!

In science class later that day, the momentum for the science fair was even stronger. Near the end of class, Mr. Moore, the girls' science teacher, passed out informational sheets printed on the back of old worksheets—Mr. Moore was totally into recycling—and told the class that they should start thinking about their projects.

"This is a revolutionary day for Abigail Adams, class. Did you hear me? Revoluuuutionary!" He sang in a silly voice, rolling his R's as the class giggled and rolled their eyes. Maeve thought Mr. Moore should join a theater group. Then he got right down to business, explaining the rules.

"Each student should choose an environmental topic that he or she is passionate about—which, judging by the enthusiasm shown at assembly today, I assume will not be difficult. Be sure to use as many recycled materials as possible in your presentations. And if you need any help, of course I am always available for consultation."

The bell rang then and Maeve started gathering her things, listening to her friends talk about their project plans. "I'm going to talk to Miss Pierce about my project tonight,"

Abigail Adams Junior High
Science Fair

Announcing a new theme:
the environment.

Go green
with AAJH!

Brought to you by
the Green Machine

Isabel M.

Charlotte was saying. "She'll probably have lots of good ideas. I feel so lucky to have a real, live scientist living right in the same house with me!"

Maeve was so relieved that Mr. Moore was willing to help them. Even though Maeve had Matt (the adorable certified science geek) to help her out, it was always reassuring to know that her teachers had her back.

"You know what, BSG?" Maeve said, draping her arms around Avery's and Charlotte's shoulders. "This science project is going to be . . . I dunno . . . fun!"

Sleepless in Scienceville

It was eleven o'clock at night, and everyone in the Summers household was sound asleep in bed. Well . . . almost everyone. Katani was still wide awake, tossing and turning. She had gone to bed more than an hour and a half before, but soon found sleeping impossible. How was she supposed to doze off to dreamland when her head was busy pumping out a million ideas a minute about the upcoming science fair? Katani didn't know what made her giddier: planning a line of clothing for her future Kgirl Enterprises or having an exciting assignment like the environmental science fair project to plan.

Right now, however, science was the only thing on her mind. She wanted her project to be totally off the hook. She wanted it to be mind-blowing. And she wanted it to impact the environment in a very real way. All she needed was the perfect idea. The question was . . . what?

Katani just couldn't take it anymore and batted down her covers, careful not to wake Kelley, who was sleeping soundly in the other twin bed. Katani threw on her terry cloth bathrobe, which she had modified by sewing on sparkly beads, tucked her feet into her slippers, and tiptoed out of the room.

Katani always felt lucky to have the parents she did, but at this moment in time she felt particularly lucky to have a father who was an electrician. Somewhere in his massive collection of tools and supplies, her father would certainly have the makings for Katani's unbelievable science fair project—something totally "revolutionary," like Mr. Moore said. The thing about being creative, Katani had learned, is that sometimes creativity could come from unusual places. And her father's garage was guaranteed to get her brain juices flowing.

A few months ago, Katani had gone on a road trip with Maeve and Maeve's dad, and on the way the car had gotten a flat tire. Ever since that incident, Katani had been determined to learn as much about electricity, cars, and plumbing as a seventh grader could know. It was part of her master plan of leading "a life of empowerment and success"—she had read all about it in this book called *Girls Gone Successful* by Brenda Bredelman, the famous female CEO. So far, she had gotten her dad to teach her how to fix the leak under the kitchen sink and how to hang a series of framed pictures in the family living room. But, hey, it was a start, right?

First things first: the Kgirl list. She found a notebook in her father's desk drawer and began writing down the names of all the supplies she might possibly be able to use for a project about electricity. Maybe a complete inventory would lead to a genius idea. "Let's see . . ." Katani whispered as she studied the words on her sheet. "Mini light bulbs . . . nails . . . wires. . . . " She was getting more excited with every word.

Her project was going to be great . . . she could just feel it.

Katani tried to be as quiet as a mouse as she jostled the garage door and crept inside. She flipped on the switch. The room was filled to the brim with wires, wood, and wall-to-wall cases of tools, all gleaming in the white light.

Suddenly, Katani dropped her notebook and let out a scream as she heard the sounds of an alarm going off. *Oh, no!* She had completely forgotten the alarm system her dad turned on in the garage at night.

"Honey? What in the name of Judge Judy is going on around here?" Katani heard her father's voice.

Slowly, Katani turned around to see her entire family filling the doorway behind her father . . . every one of them looking very confused. Kelley was shrieking, "There's an emergency, Katani. Intruder alert! Intruder alert!" Kelley must have picked that up from a commercial she had seen. She had a tendency to do that.

"Shh . . . shh. There, there, sweetie," Mrs. Summers comforted, rubbing her daughter's forehead.

"There's no intruder, Kelley," Katani's older sister Patrice said, rolling her eyes. "Katani *is* the intruder!"

Kelley knitted her brows. "Huh? Katani's intruding?"

Katani groaned. "Patrice, knock it off!" Katani rushed over and wrapped an arm around her confused sister. "I'm not intruding, Kelley. I was just trying to get ahead on a homework assignment."

"Oh, Katani." Her father couldn't help laughing. "I think it's wonderful how motivated you are about your schoolwork . . . but there are better times than the middle of the night to do research. You had the whole family thinking we were under attack. In fact, here they come. . . ." The sounds of police sirens filled the night air.

"Oops," Katani said guiltily. "I didn't mean to do that. I just wanted a head start . . ."

Katani's mother ushered Patrice and Kelley back up the stairs as Kelley joyously sang, "No intruder, no intruder!"

Her father gave Katani a warm bear hug. "Hey, kiddo, what do you say tomorrow morning you and I discuss this whole science fair project thing over breakfast? You might be surprised to find that your old man knows a thing or two about alternative energy, like wind and solar—very environmentally trendy and cool, no?"

Katani had to chuckle at her father's attempt at coolness. He might not be as "environmentally trendy" as he thought, but he did know an awful lot about electricity. "Sounds great!" she agreed. "And, Dad, would you mind if maybe tomorrow I checked out some more of this gear?"

"For my budding little scientist . . . anything!" her father said with an approving nod. "But only on one condition: no more late-night research projects. Deal?"

Katani laughed. "Deal."

When the doorbell rang, Katani ran for her bedroom and put her head under the pillow. But not before she heard her father say, "Sorry, officers. It was nice of the neighbors to call, but our 'intruder' was just a budding scientist who wanted a head start."

Katani hoped the policemen weren't blabbermouths. She would be so embarrassed if it got out that Katani Summers was caught doing homework in the middle of the night.

CHAPTER

9

A Sticky Situation

et me get this straight . . . you were breaking and entering
. . . in *your own house*?" Avery was laughing so hard that
milk had begun to drip out of her nostrils. The thought
of her completely cool, confident friend Katani caught red-
handed like some kind of criminal cracked Avery up.

Katani shook her head, making the color-coordinated
beads in her hair clatter. "Shhhh . . . I know it was bad, but
let's not announce it to the whole school. Definitely not one
of my coolest moments," Katani admitted.

"Hey, on the bright side, your mom's a lawyer right? So
she can represent you . . . *and* sue you?" Isabel joked.

"Ha ha, very funny, girls. But seriously, you have no idea
what kind of pressure I'm feeling here! I need my project to
be awesome . . . and so far all I've done is totally freak out my
family," Katani paused and let out a giant yawn, "and stayed
up way too late. But on the plus side I think I know what I
want to do my project on . . . well, kinda. My dad was telling
me some basic stuff about electricity and alternative energy

this morning. I was thinking I could look into some of those other kinds of energy sources . . . maybe. But it's gonna be tough since I don't know anything about it."

Charlotte put her hand on her friend's shoulder. "Are you kidding, Katani? You'll get this done." She picked up a pickle from her lunch tray and held it over the table. "Anyone want to trade a pickle for a cookie?" Isabel, Maeve, and Katani looked at her as if she had three heads.

"Throw in half your turkey sub and we'll call it even," Avery agreed, snatching the pickle out of Charlotte's hand.

Maeve thrust her head into her hands and grabbed at her hair in typical dramatic fashion. "Ugh! I'm the one with the extremely wonderful tutor who's a whiz at science . . . and I don't have a clue what I'm going to do my project on. I can't believe how on the ball you are already, Katani. Everybody's always ahead of me on school stuff!"

Suddenly, Katani heard the sound of snorting from the table behind them. "Katani Summers? On the ball? I thought that sports wasn't your thing."

Katani felt her blood boil, but kept her Kgirl cool and slowly turned around to see who would make such a lame remark. She found herself face-to-freckled-face with Reggie DeWitt, a.k.a Math Boy, a.k.a one of the top students in the seventh grade . . . and therefore, her academic rival. Especially since Reggie had decided he didn't want her as his partner for the big math project a few weeks ago—just because Katani forgot to show up for one little meeting. And then he acted like a total weirdo around her, even *after* Katani wrote him a really nice apology note. What*ever*. At this point, Katani really had no interest whatsoever in speaking to Mr. Reggie DeWitt at all.

But the Reggie DeWitt in front of her was definitely not the Reggie DeWitt she was used to. Katani exchanged a look with the rest of the BSG, who were all staring at Math Boy. He had always been a khakis-and-a-button-down kind of guy—but now he looked like he had walked straight off the set of a hip-hop video, wearing an oversize black hoodie with baggy jeans and a baseball cap turned slightly sideways.

"Uh, Reggie, what's with the new look?" Avery asked.

"Just a little change of pace, ladies," Reggie smoothly explained. He was eating lunch alone at a table behind them surrounded by a mountain of text books. With one slick shift, however, he was suddenly sitting backwards on his lunch chair at the BSG table, jammed smack between Avery and Katani . . . and the Kgirl was not pleased.

"Whaddya think, Katani? I know you're really into clothes and stuff," he asked, leaning in closer so she couldn't help noticing his sparkling green eyes. She suddenly flashed back to that time before she wasn't speaking to him, when they first started working on the math project, when she had noticed for the first time how cute he was . . .

Katani shook her head to get rid of all those thoughts. Reggie had dumped her, and she was mad. She frowned at him. "I don't think it's really your style," she said coldly.

Reggie seemed to lose his cool for a moment, then regrouped and went right on. "Now, I'm curious, as the founders of the Green Machine, what are you girls doing your projects on?" Reggie asked. Charlotte had to admire his recovery. Katani could freeze a cup of Montoya's hot chocolate in August with one of her stares.

"Yeah, right—like I'd tell you!" Katani balked. "There's

no way you're gonna steal *my* ideas, Reggie DeWitt."

Reggie began to laugh. "Steal your ideas? Oh, that's a good one! Brains, fashion, and a sense of humor . . . you are too much, Katani." He laughed so loud and for so long that Katani started to wonder if Reggie hadn't spent one too many hours staring at his math textbook. The girls looked at one another again, all of them thinking the same thing: *What happened to Math Boy?*

"What's so funny?" Isabel demanded. She wanted him to stop with the weird laughter.

"Nah, it's nothing," he said, catching his breath. "Just that, well, I think it's real funny that you guys suspect me of being an idea stealer. But the fact of the matter is . . . it's just not necessary. You see, science and me . . . well, it's kind of a gift. This is really embarrassing, but last year, I did this essay on how coral reefs are being destroyed by climate change, and my teacher entered it into this nationwide competition, and I came in second in the country. There was all this scholarship money involved, and I just felt so guilty about it, 'cause I just wrote the essay for fun, you know?"

The BSG looked at each other and Avery made a funny noise. "I'm sure that was really hard on you, Reg," she snorted.

"Dude!" Reggie insisted. "I felt so guilty about it. At least when I whup you all in the science fair this time"—he raised his eyebrows mischievously—"I'll be doing it on purpose."

"How kind of you," Katani said sarcastically.

Reggie folded his arms. "It is, don't you think? So tell me, Miss Summers, what is your brilliant project for the fair gonna be?"

Katani was just about to tell Reggie to leave her alone, when she heard another enthusiastic voice approaching. "Ooh, are we talking about the science fair?" It was Betsy Fitzgerald. Katani wondered why was it that when school pressure was at its worst, all the most competitive students seemed to stick to her like glue. Was there some sort of sign on her back that said "Annoy me" or something? (If so, she hoped it matched her purse!)

"I'm super-psyched about my project. I'm investigating the effects of global warming on the gray whale." Betsy also didn't wait for an invitation to sit down at the BSG table. She slung her bag on the table and continued, "Did you know that climate change is affecting their food supply? They're skinny. And did you know that brown bears in Spain are affected? And did you know that the Arctic foxes in, of course, the Arctic are affected?"

Maeve glanced at Charlotte and shook her head. If Betsy Fitzgerald ever wrote her autobiography, Maeve supposed that the title would be "Did You Know That . . . ?"

Reggie seemed to be losing interest fast, and turned his attention back to Katani. "You still haven't told me about your project, Katani. Give it up, yo."

Watching Reggie try to get under Katani's skin reminded Charlotte of how her old friend Philippe from Paris used to tease her all the time. He loved writing like Charlotte, but of course writing in French was always a little easier for a native Parisian like him than for Charlotte, whose first language was English. He liked to mimic Charlotte's grammar and point out when she used tenses incorrectly. At the time, it made her so furious. Now she could see that this was Philippe's—and

Reggie's—way of trying to flirt. If this is what boys did when they liked you, Charlotte wondered what they did when they *didn't* like you. Judging by the death stare Katani was shooting at Reggie, his flirting attempts were failing fast.

"Well, I have an idea for my project," Charlotte volunteered, hoping to divert Reggie's attention. "I want to do something on alternative energy too, Katani. I'm thinking I'll get Miss Pierce to help me, because she's an astronomer, after all. She knows so much about the stars . . . she'll be able to help me understand how our star, the sun, fuels our whole planet. Actually, I called her last night to see when she could talk to me, but she said she's busy until next week." Charlotte looked down, a little glumly. "I might try again this afternoon, though. I mean, I'm just so excited to get started!"

"That's a great idea, Char," Isabel complimented her. "I've actually done a little work on my project, too. Check this out." Isabel pulled her sketchbook out of her bag and flipped to some beautiful, green illustrations. "These are my drawings of algae. They're just some rough sketches. I'm not sure where I'm going with it yet, but I was thinking of using my art to show how global warming affects algae."

As the kids at the table oohed and aahed over Isabel's work, Maeve felt her own tongue go dry. How did her friends already have so much of their projects figured out, when she still didn't have a clue?

"Maeve? Yo—Earth to Maeve . . . is everything okay?" Avery waved her hand in front of Maeve's face.

"Huh? Oh, yeah, I'm fine," Maeve replied, blinking back to reality.

"Really?" asked Isabel. "You've been acting kind of weird

all through lunch. Are you sure there's not something bothering you?"

Isabel looked concerned. Maeve wondered if Elena Maria had mentioned their little run-in at the mall on Monday. Usually, Maeve adored being the center of attention. But right now, with not only the BSG staring at her, but Reggie and Betsy too, Maeve was not enjoying the spotlight. "I'm fine! Everything's fine. Geez . . ." she muttered, dabbing a few beads of sweat from her forehead. "Why, did someone say something?" Maeve asked Isabel softly.

Isabel looked bewildered. "Say something? Say something about what?"

"Something about . . ." Maeve's voice dropped, "*something* . . ." Maeve jerked her head and glanced around the whole table. Suddenly the whole table burst out in laughter.

"Yikes, Maeve!" Avery chuckled. "You really had me going there for a second. I say, don't worry so much about the projects, dudes. This is supposed to be *fun* on top of being all educational, remember? And I mean, I'm the one who came up with the idea for the Green Machine, and I don't even have a clue about my science fair project yet. There's just so many different things you could do a project on! Like global warming, recycling, animal habitats . . ."

While Avery rattled on and on, Maeve felt relieved that the subject had been changed to something that wasn't her, but she still wasn't 100 percent convinced that Elena Maria hadn't told Isabel about her bra. Soon enough, she knew, it would be time to come clean.

Just then, out of the corner of her eye, Charlotte noticed Anna McMasters giggling about something with Kiki

Underwood. If Anna and Joline were the Queens of Mean, Kiki was the Grand Empress of Mean. And when those girls got to chilling together, Charlotte knew they were up to no good. Using her detective skills, Charlotte pulled a small mirror from her bag to inspect the scene going on behind her.

She watched closely as Kiki handed Anna a tiny, bright blue rectangle. "This stuff is totally off the hook!" Anna squealed. She popped the little rectangle into her mouth and started chewing noisily. "I mean, it's really good," she said to Kiki through a mouth full of blue goo, "but are you sure bubble gum is . . . like . . . cool?"

Charlotte watched Kiki narrow her eyes at Anna. Then she shrugged and started casually putting her stuff back into her purse. "Whatever, Anna. If you don't want to be on top of this trend, that's fine with me. I'm sure there are tons of other girls in our class who want to be official Tru Blu Promotion Girls."

"No no no no no," Anna replied quickly, smacking the gum even harder and faster. "You're so right! This gum is totally hot!" She jumped up and marched right over to stand near the BSG table. "Everyone wants to know where I got it, Kiks!"

Kiki cackled delightedly. "Oh, there is a whole big bag where this came from, girlfriend. This gum is so delish, and it blows the biggest bubbles. It hasn't been released to stores yet, but when it does, can you imagine how *huge* it'll be? Plus, with Jake Axle endorsing this? We're going to be unstoppable!"

Charlotte snapped her mirror shut, realizing that spying wasn't really spying if the people you were spying on *wanted* to be spied on. She made a note to write that one down, as it would make a fabulous tongue twister.

"This new deal with the gum factory is going to make your dad filthy rich," Anna gushed. "You could like have your own yacht or something."

"My dad and me rock," Kiki added, shooting the BSG a glance to make sure they were listening. "I love my life!" she sang as she and Anna skipped away.

"Gum factory?" Avery looked around the table suspiciously. "What the heck was that about?"

Reggie chortled. "Don't you girls read the paper? There was a huge article in the newspaper just two days ago. You know Kiki Underwood's dad is a manager for rock bands, right? He manages Jake Axle. Well, he made a deal with this huge bubble gum factory that's about to open here in Boston, and Jake Axle is endorsing the product. His new song, "I Am Rubber, You Are Glue" is going to be on all the gum commercials. I mean, not that I listen to pop music, but—"

"Gum factory!" Avery cried in outrage. "Gum factory? Another factory spewing toxic chemicals into the air is the last thing Boston needs. Did you guys know about this?"

Betsy Fitzgerald folded her arms. "Are you kidding? I pride myself on staying on top of all current events: global, national, and *especially* local. This factory is nowhere near the T and no buses go there, so there'll be lots of commuters' cars pumping more fossil fuel fumes into the air. And the real problem is that Tru Blu is totally overpackaged—wrappers over wrappers over wrappers. It's so not Green. But . . . I don't know about toxic chemicals, Avery. I didn't read anything in the paper about their carbon emissions or—"

"Carbon emissions? What's that?"

Betsy smiled and leaned back in her chair. She loved being asked to explain things. "Well, you see, Avery, producing energy from fossil fuels releases CO_2, you know, carbon dioxide, into the air—"

"And that factory is going to use a ton of energy!" Avery shouted, without bothering to listen to the rest of what Betsy was saying. She was getting more pumped about the issue by the second.

"That's not really what I was going to say—" Betsy started.

Katani shifted uncomfortably in her chair. "Actually . . ." she began. "Oh, never mind."

"What?" Avery asked.

Katani shrugged, "Well, it's just that, maybe this factory isn't necessarily a bad thing. I mean, it's bringing business to the city. They've even hired my dad to do some work, and he didn't mention anything about the factory being a big polluter. He thinks it could really help out the local economy."

"Economy-shmonomy!" Avery cried. "All those wrappers mean fewer trees to absorb some of the CO_2. More commuters equals more CO_2 in the air!" She jumped out of her chair and shouted, "Stop the factory!" while pumping one fist into the air.

Several kids from the next table over turned around to see who was rallying for the environment in the middle of the cafeteria. The BSG looked at Avery in surprise. "Are you turning into me?" Maeve asked. "Because that speech was definitely stage-worthy, Avery."

"I think you're taking this a little too far," the sensible Charlotte commented.

I couldn't agree more, Katani thought. "People need to work so they can eat," she told Avery, feeling the blood rise to her face.

Lucky for everyone, the final lunch bell sounded. Maeve had never felt so relieved for her social time to be over. The BSG shuffled out, feeling less on the same environmental page at the end of lunch than they had at the beginning. As for Maeve, she was feeling anxious. *Science is too hard,* she thought. *Way too hard.*

Tru Blu Goo

As the day went on, things went from bad to worse. Before science class began, Avery watched kids surround Kiki, Joline, and Anna, dying to get their paws on the brand new Tru Blu Gum. "I heard that this is the only gum that Jake Axle chews!" Samantha Simmons gushed at Kiki.

"It's true," Kiki confirmed. "He says it helps him sing better."

"Oh, my *gosh* that is *so cool!*" Samantha cried, eagerly munching her gum.

Avery rolled her eyes, but she couldn't help feeling a tad jealous. Just a couple days ago, everyone had been crowded around *her,* getting pumped about the Green Machine. Now they were all into . . . blue bubble gum? "This is unbelievable! Everyone thinks Kiki Underwood is soooo cool just because she gives out a few pieces of free gum. Totally lame. Who cares about Tru Blu Goo, or whatever it's called? We gotta get people to focus on what's really important—saving this planet!"

"Don't sweat it, Avery," said Isabel, trying to cheer her

friend up. "This gum thing is only a fad. And we all know that fads don't stick for long."

"Ew!" Charlotte suddenly screeched. "There's something on me!" Charlotte tried to stand, but her jeans were glued to her seat.

Avery scuttled over to inspect. "Gross! It's Tru Blu Gum, Char. Someone left it on your chair."

Charlotte turned beet red, experiencing another one of her infamous moments of public humiliation. She tried to pry the sticky goop off her jeans, but it just wouldn't give. "I can't believe this." She gulped. "And these pants are brand new."

"I can put a cool patch over the gum spot if you want," Katani offered.

"Thanks," replied Charlotte. "That might help, I guess."

Later in class, Chelsea Briggs found a piece of Tru Blu sticking to the elbow of her jacket. "Gross!" she whispered to Isabel, who very much agreed. "This stuff is super sticky. If I find the gum leprechaun that stuck this on me, there's going to be trouble."

"I'm with you, Chels," Isabel whispered back. "But the QOM handed out free samples to *every*one, so it's probably *every*where! Double ew."

When the bell rang at the end of class, Avery was the first kid out of her seat and dashing toward the hallway. But half-way out the door, she was stopped dead in her tracks. One of her cherished, bright orange sneakers—the ones she had paid for herself with all the money she earned walking dogs in the neighborhood last summer—was stuck fast to the tiled floor of the science room.

The BSG stood frozen in a semi-circle in front of her,

terrified that Avery might morph into a cannonball and go charging straight for Kiki.

"Now, Ave," Charlotte said in her most soothing voice, "don't get mad . . ."

Avery's response was even more intense than the girls could have predicted. "Mad? Mad?" Avery squeaked in a loud, tight voice. "Oh, I'm not mad. This is *no* time to get mad . . . it's time to get *even*." Avery pointed at her sneaker and the disgusting elastic strip of gum stretching up and down as she raised and lowered her foot. "This, my friends, is war!" she declared. And with that pronouncement, Avery charged down the hall.

Charlotte glanced at the rest of the BSG. "Um, should we be worried here?"

Maeve shrugged. "I don't know. It's Avery, and you know how she gets. I mean this could be a good thing. If she's going to be an environmental warrior, maybe she needs to power up. Isn't that what the Green Machine is all about?"

Her friends weakly nodded, but they were still uncertain. What if the Green Machine got clobbered by . . . the *Blue* Machine?

CHAPTER

10

Cramping the Kgirl Style

I'm gonna go make sure she doesn't try to make a bubble the size of Texas and blow it at Kiki's face," Isabel decided.

"Good idea!" Charlotte agreed.

"I gotta go, anyway," said Maeve, following Isabel and Charlotte into the hall. "I have a tutoring session with Matt in an hour. You coming, Katani?" Maeve called behind her.

Katani shuffled her feet and glanced back into the empty classroom where Mr. Moore sat at his desk grading papers. "I just have to ask Mr. Moore a quick question. You guys go ahead. I'll catch up later."

She was secretly thrilled to have the chance to pick Mr. Moore's brain about her science fair project. She would have explained this to the BSG, but she had a feeling that sometimes her super-intense study habits stressed out her BFFs . . . especially Maeve.

Mr. Moore was exactly one inch shorter than Katani with very short brown hair and a big-time love of plaid, short-sleeved shirts, and cows. The entire room was decorated with cow stuff, from the paper towel dispenser to the frames on the pictures on Mr. Moore's desk. Thankfully, he did not let his cow obsession interfere with his other love—science—of which he was a good and very patient instructor.

"Hello, Katani. Is there something I can help you with?"

"Yes. Mr. Moore, I've been doing a lot of thinking about my science fair project, and I had a few concerns."

Mr. Moore looked puzzled. "My, Katani! Your grades this semester have been stellar. I'm sure you have absolutely nothing to worry about."

Katani sighed. How was it that even her teachers didn't understand her drive to succeed? "Oh, it's not my grade I'm worried about, Mr. Moore. I mean, I know that if I work really hard, I can do fine and everything. It's just that, well, I was thinking about doing a project about electricity, right? But now the theme of the science fair is the environment . . . which obviously I'm totally cool with. I mean, my friends and I were sort of the ones who started the whole environment theme in the first place . . ."

Mr. Moore closed his eyes and rubbed his forehead. "Sorry, Katani . . . I'm not following."

"Well, I started off wanting to do something about electricity—'cause my dad's an electrician—but then my dad told me all this stuff about alternative energy that sounded really cool. But my friend Charlotte is already doing solar energy . . . so now I just don't know what to do!" Yikes. Katani realized that saying her thoughts out loud was even stressing *her* out! Poor Mr. Moore.

Her good-natured teacher just laughed, however, and reached into the lower drawer of his cow-decorated desk.

"Okay, here we go—my secret stash of books. I think you're on the right track here, Katani. And don't worry. Besides solar, there are plenty of other kinds of alternate energy—energy that doesn't come from people burning fossil fuels like coal and oil. Why don't you browse through these and see what you can find? Then come back to me if you have questions, okay?"

"Thanks!" Katani said. She had no idea where to begin with the heavy textbooks. She dropped them on a desk and took a seat. The pile of books was so high, it towered over her head. This was not going to be easy. She took a deep breath, and was getting ready to dive in, when—

"Yo, what's up Mr. M?"

Katani peeked up from over the books. "Oh, pleeease!" she groaned under her breath. It was Reggie DeWitt. Katani shrank back behind the books and pretended not to notice him.

"So I've been making mad progress on ideas for my fair project," Reggie gloated, glancing over at Katani to make sure she heard him, "and I just wanted to shoot some of my thought waves by you. After all, you are the science whiz of AAJH!"

Katani wanted to disappear. Whatever he was trying to pull with this new "super fly" persona, Reggie was still a total geek! He and Betsy Fitzgerald would really make a great match, she thought. Well, except that if you didn't know any better, you'd think that Reggie was a rap superstar by the way he was dressed. Betsy was far from rap superstar style.

"You kids are too much!" remarked Mr. Moore. "Katani here came to me for the same thing."

Katani peered out from behind the books and gave Reggie a dry smile.

"K-Summers . . . no way," Reggie said with a chuckle. "I shoulda known I'd find you here. Well, you know what they say—great minds think alike."

Katani rolled her eyes. Was that his own back-handed way of calling *himself* a genius?

"But wait," Reggie said, "I thought you didn't know what you were going to do yet, Katani? I mean, isn't that what you said at lunch?"

"For your information, Reggie, it just so happens—"

"I gave her some books from my treasure chest to help jump-start her creativity," Mr. Moore explained.

Katani really wished the tiles in the floor would open up and swallow her whole. *Thanks a lot, Mr. Moore,* she thought to herself.

"MOOooo . . . MOOooo . . . MOOooo!" went the cell phone on Mr. Moore's desk.

Mr. Moore laughed. "Oops. Hold on guys, it's my wife. Reggie . . . um, I'll be with you in a sec," Mr. Moore promised, flipping open his phone and wandering into the hallway. "Hello, muffin!"

Katani watched Reggie strut sickeningly over to her desk. He pushed the books aside and gave Katani a wide smile from ear to ear. "Soooo . . . any thoughts?"

Katani shot him a death stare. "MYOB, Reggie."

"Hey, hey, hey, now. Take it easy. I'm just trying to help." He took the Joe Dude sunglasses from his forehead and pushed them onto his nose. "Is it hot in here, or is it just me?"

That was just *too* much. Who did he think he was? "As much as I appreciate your," Katani crunched her fingers into two quotation marks, "help, I think I can handle this project perfectly well on my own, thank you *very* much. Besides, my dad's an electrician, so any questions I have, I'll probably just take to him. . . . After all, he *is* a professional."

"Well, let's just see what you got." Reggie pushed his sun-glasses back up, walked behind Katani, and leaned in way too close over her shoulder to read her notes. "Build your own electric car . . . Hey, I did something like that back in fifth grade!"

Katani slammed her notebook shut. "That's it! No way you're reading my notes, Reggie."

Reggie laughed. "What, do you think I'm going to copy you? Katani, I'm already halfway done with plans for my whole project. Trust me, I *don't* need to copy *you*." He leaned in again and tried to pry the notebook open. His face was so close to Katani's she could smell his lotion. She felt her cheeks grow warm, and with all her might, grabbed the notebook from his hands. Reggie lost his balance and nearly knocked over a tray of test tubes on the lab table behind him.

"Oh, Reggie," she gasped. She hadn't meant to knock him over.

"Sheesh, Katani," he said as he struggled to regain his balance. Then he seemed to remember that he was supposed to be Mr. Cool. "I mean, uh . . . yo, Katani! I'm just . . . uh . . . joking with you, girl."

"Yeah, well, sometimes people don't like to be joked with!" Katani huffed. "Especially when they are trying to work!" She felt her voice cracking. She was mad at Reggie, but even more mad at herself for getting so upset. Reggie was telling the truth . . . he hadn't really done anything at all. But the more he stood there wearing his dumb sunglasses and his puffy, black sneakers looking like he thought he was just some kind of gift to mankind . . . the more frustrated she felt herself becoming. Just because he was smart, and a whiz at math, and so adorable. . . . Katani gasped, suddenly realizing the thought that had just crossed her mind. *Adorable? Who am I, Maeve??*

"What's bugging you, Kgirl?" Reggie asked.

"Nothing!" Katani snapped, then took a breath and composed herself. In a calmer voice she tried again. "I mean, nothing. Sorry, I'm just a little stressed over this project thing. Sorry to be such a . . ."

Reggie gave her a half smile. "Maniac?"

Katani grinned. "Yeah. Or something. I gotta run, Reggie . . . my friends are waiting. Tell Mr. Moore I'm borrowing the book with the red cover, okay?" She shoved the book in her backpack and took off out the door. But on the way out, she felt something holding her shoe to the floor.

"Oh, please!" Katani moaned, yanking her foot up off the floor. "Enough with this Tru Blu stupidity already!"

"Hey, Katani, you forgot your . . . ," Reggie hollered behind her, but she was long gone. "Scarf," he mumbled, placing the yellow fabric in his duffel.

Part Two
Bubble Gum Wars

11

Three Peonies in a Pod

Maeve, are you ready for Matt?" Maeve's mother called down the hall. "Have you got your math groove on?"

"Almost!" Maeve shouted between giggles. Her mother could be so weird sometimes.

What her mom really meant, Maeve knew, was did she have all of her books and papers ready . . . had she gone over the material beforehand . . . had she done as much of her homework as possible so Matt could swoop in and conveniently fill in the blanks. Of course what *Maeve* meant by ready was . . . was her light pink blush shimmering on her cheeks just so to give her a lovely glow?

Maeve ran a tube of glitter gloss over her mouth. "There," she said, pleased with what she saw in the reflection. She studied her entire outfit. She'd changed out of her school clothes into a pink terry cloth track suit—the kind that all the celebs in her *Teen Beat* magazine were wearing. Underneath her hoodie, she was wearing a lime green T-shirt. The green shade went wonderfully with her red hair and blue eyes.

"'Kay, Mom, I'm ready!" Maeve grabbed her backpack, which for the first time in her life was pretty much in order. *Maybe watching all those science girls at the festival has inspired me*, she thought as she headed to the kitchen. "Mmm . . . something smells fabuloso in here, Mom. What is that?"

Ms. Kaplan furrowed her brows. "Angel hair pasta with marinara . . . um, Maeve, where do you think you're going . . . a rock concert?"

"Um, nooo . . ." Maeve replied innocently, spreading out her schoolwork neatly—for her—on the kitchen table.

"So then why do you look like you're about to take a glamour-shot for that *Teen Beat* magazine?"

"Do I?" Maeve giggled as she caught a glimpse of her reflection in the china cabinet.

"You do." Ms. Kaplan poured the pasta into a colander and shook out the excess water. "Maeve, honey, I don't care what you wear to study, but Matt is here to help you with schoolwork. You need to be prepared."

"Well, obviously . . ."

"And you know that the most important thing should be that you have all your math and science work ready . . . not your hair. Right?"

Maeve shrugged. "Duh, Mom."

Ms. Kaplan kissed her daughter's forehead. "Just checking." She poured the marinara sauce into the pot with the pasta. "Sam and I are going to have an early dinner in the other room so we don't interrupt you guys." As she walked out of the kitchen she heard her daughter singing "Hopelessly Devoted to You" from *Grease*. "Oy . . . ," Ms. Kaplan mumbled.

Maeve stared at her books and pink, glow-in-the-dark pens all lined up on the table. Something was missing. She needed something . . . atmospheric. "That's it!" Maeve said out loud, catching sight of the tiny log cabin on the window ledge. She lit the scent cone inside and very soon the entire kitchen smelled like pine needles and Vermont fireplaces. "Absolutely *Little Women* perfect!" she decided. It was just the way she imagined the cozy family home in the movie of *Little Women* would smell. The original vintage version of course, with Katharine Hepburn as Jo March. It was one of Maeve's favorite classic romantic movies of all time.

When the doorbell rang, Maeve jumped up to greet Matt.

"Mix-Master-Curl, MK-T!" Matt cried, slapping Maeve five. "Wow, Maeve. You look very . . . pink. Even more than usual. That can't be easy."

"Ha ha, it wasn't!" Maeve laughed—maybe a little too hard.

Matt took a seat at the table. "Okay, great news. Bailey gave me some awesome science project ideas . . . ah—aah—*choo*!" Matt sneezed so hard it nearly knocked him off the chair.

"Bless you!" Maeve cried, leaping up to find him a tissue. Hearing Bailey's name out loud made Maeve feel like she needed to move around.

"Thanks. As I was saying, I think that doing a project on the plants would be a great idea for you. When I was in high school I . . . ah—aah—*aah—choo*!"

Maeve gave him another tissue. Matt sniffled. "What is that? I smell pine needles."

"Well, yeah . . . I lit the scent cone in our little log house. . . ." Maeve pointed to the window ledge. "I thought it would smell Vermont-y."

Matt covered his nose with the tissue. "Pine!" he exclaimed. "I'm very allergic to pine. First it starts with sneezing, then I break out in hives." Maeve quickly ran over to the window and ran the whole house under the faucet. Just to be safe, she put it outside on the fire escape to dry. Matt went on, "Wow, that was incredibly uncomfortable."

Maeve felt a little embarrassed as she skulked back to the table. *Guess my domestic goddess-ing skills still need a little work,* she thought. "Is that better?"

Matt nodded and dabbed his eyes. "Yes. Sorry. Thanks. Now, let's get started. I noticed that at the festival you had a little spark when we were looking at the exhibit on peonies and organic fertilizer."

Maeve's face lit up and she forgot all about Bailey and Matt for the moment. Those peonies *had* spoken to her at the festival. She could practically smell their aroma now. "Matt, those flowers were so beautiful. Isn't it funny how things start off small and plain, like bulbs and seeds? Then it's like, overnight, there's a beautiful pink flower! I don't think I have ever seen a flower as beautiful as a peony. I think peonies are even more beautiful than roses," she rhapsodized.

"Yeah, they are pretty cool looking," a less-dramatic Matt answered. Maeve blinked away her mood-setting fumble with the incense and concentrated all her energy on what Matt was saying. She wondered if he noticed how grown-up she seemed. Besides, plants were more interesting than math problems.

"But it's not exactly overnight, Maeve. Every day plants grow very, very slowly. It's hard to tell that they've changed at all sometimes."

Maeve twirled a ringlet around her pencil. It really wasn't hard for her to act like she was paying attention, because what Matt was saying was actually pretty interesting. It was neat to think about those little baby peonies growing up into beautiful blossoms providing perfume to the world. A science project on flowers might actually be . . . *fun*.

"But they do grow up . . . the plants," she said. "As long as they have enough love, proper light, water and food, right?"

"Exactly!" Matt exclaimed. "Maeve, I think we're totally on the same page here!"

Maeve knew she must be absolutely glowing. "We are?" Had Matt finally picked up her hints that she was worlds more mature than most seventh graders . . . that she was practically a full-fledged teenager?

Matt ruffled his hair. "Yup. My girlfriend was right. She thought that a plant-growth experiment would be just perfect for you. She said she thought you might have the soul of a botanist."

Botanist! Really? But Maeve's moment of excitement quickly turned to despair. *Girlfriend?*

"Bailey is your girlfriend?" she spit out.

Two red circles appeared on Matt's cheeks. "Well . . . *yeah*. At first we were just pals, you know? Then we realized that we had a lot in common. We both love science. She got me involved in the whole eco movement. She's got a cool laugh, and a beautiful voice . . . she sings in a science a cappella group at MIT called 'Sonic Pollution' . . . isn't that funny?" A smitten Matt seemed overcome with the fabulous Bailey.

"Adorable," Maeve grumbled, shoving an Oreo into her mouth.

"And you know what I like most about her?" asked Matt.

"Her, um, unique sense of style?" Maeve suggested. She knew that might have been a little mean, but she couldn't help it. How could Matt go and get a girlfriend behind her back when it was so obvious that the perfect woman for him was *her* . . . not *Bailey*.

"Yeah, you noticed that, too."

Maeve nodded miserably. "Uh-huh."

"But no. To be honest, I really couldn't care less about clothes. What I like the most about Bailey is how thoughtful she is. Did you know that after she met you and your friends at the Sally Ride Science Festival she went to the trouble of putting together a few preliminary ideas for projects that you, Maeve, would be interested in?"

Maeve looked up. "She did?" It was bad enough that Bailey was a part of Matt's life, but now she was becoming a part of Maeve's science fair project. But she did need a project . . . *and it was kind of nice of her to think about a project for me*, a suddenly confused Maeve tried to reason.

"Yeah. When Bailey noticed how much you loved the flowers, she figured maybe you could use her organic fertilizer. Your work would help her research, and the environment, too."

"Huh? How can I help the environment? Make plants more beautiful?" Maeve was baffled.

"Well, there's that, too. But even better, trees and plants

give off oxygen and take in some of the CO_2 from the air. Too much CO_2 in the atmosphere is causing big problems, like global warming. Plus, with Bailey's organic fertilizer you avoid pesticides that can get absorbed into the earth and into our water supply."

Maeve couldn't believe that growing beautiful flowers could help protect the environment, but if it could, she definitely wanted to be part of it! "Count me in," she said finally.

"Great! I know Bailey would love to help you out with that. Listen, here is Bailey's phone number. She said if you want to, you can call her tonight and she'll help you decide on a project. She's happy to meet with you at her lab this week too."

"That's so nice," said Maeve, her voice cracking. The love of her life's girlfriend was going to help her? There was something wrong with that picture.

"So . . . should I tell her to expect your call?" asked Matt.

Maeve managed a weak, "Sure." She supposed if there was a smart college girl willing to help her, she should probably take her up on it. Maeve knew that putting together a science project would be a serious challenge for her. And Matt was right . . . it was very sweet of Bailey. But still . . . she couldn't believe that her dream boy had found a dream girl, and *it wasn't her*. It felt like her heart was going to burst into a million pieces.

CHAPTER

12

Advice—Think Twice

Ever since Charlotte Ramsey was a little girl, she had always loved looking at the night sky. It made her feel like she was part of something much bigger than just her house, her town, even her country, or her planet. The stars went on forever and ever . . . Charlotte wondered just what was out there. Plus, the stars were so beautiful they always took her breath away, as they sparkled against the black blanket of night in their reliable constellations. To Charlotte, the stars were like old friends, always waiting in the sky to greet her at the end of a long day.

There was one very important star that got a lot of attention, and it was that star that Charlotte wanted to do her science project on: the sun. It made perfect sense to Charlotte that the enormous star that all our solar system's planets orbited around would be the star to give energy and life to everything on Earth.

But she couldn't for the life of her think of a really great idea, and she was starting to panic. She really wanted to understand solar energy and how it could be part of solving global warming. She had been intrigued by the model car powered by solar energy, but she wanted to do something original, something creative. Something to go along with the cool "solar power" T-shirt she wanted to design. Katani would be so proud of her when she heard her idea.

Luckily for Charlotte, she lived right above a woman who was a real, live astronomer. Not only that, but an astronomer who was one of the nicest, sweetest ladies ever. After Charlotte had gone over her brainstorming list for the umpteenth time and decided she was completely and utterly stuck, she made up her mind to head downstairs and consult the expert. Charlotte didn't even need to cross her fingers that Miss Pierce would be in, because Miss Pierce was *always* in during the day. Her work started when the stars came out. Her life was astronomy and making amazing cookies; the astronomer was also a truly wonderful baker.

Charlotte rang Miss Pierce's bell and waited impatiently. She was so excited to hear everything Miss Pierce knew about the sun that she was practically jumping from side to side.

"Good afternoon, Charlotte. I'm so sorry, was I supposed to watch Marty today?" asked Miss Pierce with an apologetic laugh. Miss Pierce had taken quite a liking to the little dude. How could she not? It was pretty much a universal fact that the Marty Man was positively irresistible.

"No, no, not at all!" Charlotte exclaimed. "Marty's upstairs, napping in my dad's office. Actually, I'm here to ask you a few quick questions about my school science project. It's an environmental theme, and I want to do something about solar energy, but I just don't know what . . . and I've been racking my brain for hours. I promise it won't take but a few minutes. Really." She gave her mentor a hopeful look.

"Well, Charlotte, I am very busy with some calculations . . . but . . . I always have a few minutes for scientific inquiries." Miss Pierce broke into a warm smile. "Come on in. I just made some banana bread. Would you like a piece?"

Charlotte clapped. "Ooh, yum! I was wondering what that delicious smell might be!" Miss Pierce moved a giant pile of books and papers off the cozy sofa so Charlotte could sit down, then went into the kitchen. While she was gone, Charlotte looked at Miss Pierce's rows and rows of books. One book, called *Stargazers Through Time*, especially caught her eye. The title sounded interesting, but not as interesting as the author: Dr. Sapphire Pierce!

Miss Pierce came back with a giant slice of banana bread slathered in honey. "Here you go, dear. Ruby just shared this recipe with me recently. It's from her family, I believe." Miss Pierce and Katani's grandmother, Ruby Fields, were lifelong friends and the founders of the original Beacon Street Girls . . . many years ago.

Charlotte bit into the moist, sweet bread. "This is delicious!" Then she held up the book she'd found and grinned. "Thank you, *Dr.* Pierce. You never told me you were a PhD— and a writer, too! Are you famous?"

Miss Pierce just smiled. "I know many scientists who are also writers, Charlotte," she said simply. 'It's very important not only to do valuable work, but to be able to explain it to others. Science and writing can go hand in hand . . . something I'm sure a budding young writer/scientist like you is already discovering."

Charlotte nodded. "So ask me your questions," Miss Pierce went on. "You need to do a science fair project, and it must be environmentally focused. . . ."

"Exactly," Charlotte affirmed. "I'd like to do something

about solar energy, because, you know—my love for the sky. The only problem is I want my project to be unique. It seems like all the solar projects for kids I can find are like building model solar cars."

A wide grin graced Miss Pierce's face. "Ah. You're interested in photovoltaics. I might have a book or two—"

Charlotte shook her head and interrupted. "No, Miss Pierce . . . this is supposed to be environmentally-themed. On solar energy."

"Charlotte, dear," Miss Pierce explained, "photovoltaics literally means 'light electricity.' People convert the sun's energy into electricity using photovoltaic cells. You might know them as solar panels."

"I think I've heard of them," Charlotte said, a little embarrassed that she had jumped in and cut Miss Pierce off. "Miss Pierce, I'm sorry. It's just that Avery has been sending me all these articles on the rain forest and I really thought I should get started on saving the planet," she apologized.

Miss Pierce smiled kindly. "That is an admirable aim for a young scientist . . . and for an old one like me. Let's put our heads together and see if we can come up with something creative. Show me what you've got so far."

Charlotte breathed a sigh of relief as she pulled out her brainstorming notebook. With Miss Pierce on her team, she just knew her project would be great!

Gumming It Up

Avery was the fastest runner in Ms. R's class. She knew this because she made a point of challenging everyone to a race whenever she got a chance, and so far, no one had beaten her. Lucky for her, because Avery was very late. She'd stopped on her way home to get supplies for her brainstorm.

She sprinted home faster than she knew her legs could move. She arrived on the steps of the Maddens' large, colonial-style house and checked her stopwatch. "Four minutes and seventeen seconds! *Whooo-hoo!* That's an Avery Madden record!" She bolted up the stairs, taking them two at a time, burst into her bedroom, and collapsed on her bed. "I'M BEAT!" she shouted.

"Knock, knock," Scott said, rapping on her open door.

Avery turned her head so she could see her brother and squinted one eye at him. "You may enter."

"Hey . . . you're totally late, but it's cool. Mom's running late too."

"Thanks, *Dad*," Avery chided sarcastically, dragging herself up until she was sitting cross-legged on the bed. "I already called Mom's cell. So you don't need to *worry* about me." Avery dumped out the contents of her grocery bag and spread them out over her comforter. There was a Make Your Own Chewing Gum kit from Glee Gum, confectioner's sugar, rice syrup, and lots of different brands of gum.

"What's all that?" asked Scott. He picked up a piece of watermelon flavor BubbleFun and began to rip open the package.

"Hey! What do you think you're doing? Gimme that!" Avery cried, snatching the gum from her brother's hand.

"Easy, killer. I just wanted a piece of gum. What's the big deal, anyway? You have like, five *hundred* packages!" Scott grumbled.

"It just so happens these are for school. My science fair project grade depends on it, Scott, so keep your *paws off*!"

"Okay, okay . . . ," Scott mumbled. "So . . . science fair. You get some good ideas at that festival the other day?"

Avery shrugged. "Yep, and I got more ideas from the Queens of Mean, who think that Tru Blu Gum is more important than the health of the planet." Avery's brainstorm, inspired by Kiki Underwood and her minions, was to create her own brand of gum made from natural ingredients that could out-taste that Tru Blu ickiness Kiki was promoting. She wanted to make it in the shape of a long roll so that people could break off one piece at a time, with no need for all that individual packaging that would just end up in a landfill somewhere.

"So you had fun at the festival, huh?" asked Scott.

"Oh, yeah! Wicked fun. There was this awesome thing where you could make your own slime. Mine turned out to be—"

"So, uh, you think your friends had a good time?" Scott interrupted. "You know, Maeve . . . Elena Maria . . ."

Avery let out a huge groan and looked up from her gum. "I know you like Elena, Scott."

Scott looked appalled. "Oh, no way. No. I mean, she's a cool girl and all, but like—"

Avery rolled her eyes. "You mean, besides the fact that you two were making goo-goo eyes at each other like aaaaall day . . ."

"We were not—"

Avery put a hand in the air. "Dude! Get real. Besides the eye thing, besides the way you were like staring at her on the

T, besides the whole you-both-go-ape-over-cooking thing . . . Scott, it's okay if you like Elena Maria. Really."

Scott shook his head, looking down and turning red. "Well, maybe . . ." he started weakly, then trailed off.

Avery shrugged. "Hey, I'm just telling it like it is."

Scott sat down on the bed beside Avery. "So what am I supposed to do? Elena Maria is still dating that dork-face."

"That guy Jimmy."

"Ugh, I hate that dude. He's like a total washout who happens to think he is so cool because he is on the indoor lacrosse team."

Avery pinched her nose and said in a voice that sounded freakishly similar to their mother, "Now, Scott. Hate is a very negative and unpleasant word."

Scott groaned. "I very, very, very strongly dislike him. He's not good for Elena and I don't know what she sees in him."

Avery let out a long sigh. "Now, I'm seriously no expert on . . . you know . . . the love-bug thing. I actually think it's a huge snooze-fest."

Scott stood up. "Fine, fine, I get it. I'm going."

"Hold on, dude! Even though the whole romance thing gives me a headache, because you're my brother, and I think you and Elena Maria would probably be perfect for each other . . . I'm gonna help you."

Scott smiled. "That's my sis!"

"But if you tell anyone that I am playing matchmaker . . . bleeeegchy . . . well, the consequences will be dire, got it?"

"Yeah, yeah, I got it."

Avery unwrapped the watermelon gum and popped out a piece for Scott and a piece for herself. "Here. I guess I can spare *one* piece for you. Now, listen up. According to Isabel, Elena Maria and Jimmy are sort of on the rocks."

"They are?"

"Yup. Isabel says he's only interested in talking about himself, and Elena Maria is getting fed up with him. He doesn't call when he says he will . . . he blows her off to hang out with his friends . . . he gets really grouchy . . . it's not good."

"Awesome!" Scott exclaimed. "I mean . . . that's so sad for her . . ."

Avery continued. "Look. I'm gonna get to the point here. It's really easy. Maeve is like an expert on romance, right? I mean, she's definitely done her homework with all those romantic old movies she watches. So anyway, Maeve says there's one major thing that stops guys and girls from getting together . . ."

"Bad breath?" Scott blew into his hand. "Phew, watermelon."

"Nooooo! For a guy to date a girl, *he needs to ask her*!"

Scott gazed off into nothing and echoed, "He needs to ask her. Whoa. You know what, Avery? That's so crazy it just might work. So how do I ask her?"

Avery covered her eyes with her fists. "You can't ask her yet, she has a boyfriend. Ugh, even *I* know that much."

"But I thought—"

"*No.* First you have to make her see that you would be a much cooler boyfriend than Jimmy. Then she will dump Jimmy, leaving room for you to swoop in like a knight in shining whatever and win her heart."

"I could totally manage that!" Scott grinned as he threw a foam ball at his sister's head.

"Well," Avery said with a smug smile as she dodged the ball, "I am sort of a genius."

"I'm gonna start by making her my double-chocolate nut cupcakes . . . I mean, you like those, right? And you're a girl."

Avery shook her head. "Maybe you should start a little smaller, okay? Try hanging out with her. Call her. IM her. Not too much all at once. Like save the cupcakes for week two. Then when she realizes that you are paying more attention to her than her own boyfriend, the work will be practically done for you."

"Ave, you really are a genius," Scott said, nodding seriously as he processed Avery's advice. "Game on. Thanks, shortie."

Avery gave him a thumbs-up. "No prob, Bob." She felt a little weird giving advice to her older brother—especially about all that lovey-dovey stuff—but it was also kind of cool to be able to help him out.

Scott opened the door and then, turning back added, "Oh, do me a favor? Don't, um, mention this to your friends, okay?"

Avery placed her hand on her chest. "Cross my heart, hope to die, stick a needle in my soccer ball."

"Nice rhyme."

Avery shrugged. "I couldn't live without my soccer ball. That's how you know your secret's safe."

CHAPTER

13

Enough Already

Isabel adjusted the microscope and squeezed her right eye
shut. "There," she murmured. "Whoa . . ." She could not
believe how many times she'd gone to ponds and icked her
way around the green matter that floated at the top. "To think
. . . all this time there were beautiful pictures hidden in that
slime. . . ." She sighed and turned her attention to the sketchbook and colored pencils on her desk.

She'd already filled up six full pages with her detailed
sketches. Contained in the microscopic algae were incredible shapes and patterns—everything from delicate shells
that reminded her of lace to balls that looked like they were
made of Lifesavers to little half moons, all revealed under the
microscope. Isabel was mesmerized by Mother Nature's abil-
ity to showcase her secret artistic streak in something as vital
to the planet as these phytoplankton. And they had all kinds
of strange names, some of which Isabel couldn't even pro-
nounce. Diatoms, coccolithophores, dinoflagellates, desmids,
prymnesiophytes, prochlorophyte . . . who knew?

She carefully dismantled the microscope, which Emily Sullivan had been generous enough to lend her when Aunt Lourdes took her to visit Emily's lab at MIT earlier that afternoon. "Sorry guys—you can pose for me again tomorrow!" she signed off to her slides.

"Hey Iz, who're you talking to?" asked Elena Maria, suddenly appearing in the frame of their bedroom door.

"Oh! Um, no one . . . just myself," Isabel fibbed, feeling slightly ridiculous being caught talking to microscopic pond scum. "Why? What's up?"

"Nothing. I just baked some empanadas. You want?" Elena Maria walked over holding a plate of steamy, sticky pastries shaped like half-moons. The aroma of baked apple and cinnamon filled Isabel's nose.

"Ooh . . . yes, please!" Isabel took a huge bite, and goo dribbled out of the empanada and onto her chin. "*Hot!*" she cried.

"I just took them out of the oven, silly. Here." Elena Maria thrust a paper towel at her little sister, and watched, slightly disgusted, as Isabel spat out the half-chewed food.

"Sorry," Isabel squeaked. "It was really good, though!"

Elena Maria's brow wrinkled and she looked down sadly.

"Elena, did you hear me? I said they were really good! Just, you know, a little hot." Isabel smiled, but her sister still looked sad. Elena Maria wiped a tiny tear out of the corner of her eye. "Hey . . ." Isabel put her arm around Elena Maria's shoulder. "I said sorry . . ."

Elena Maria sighed. "It's not the empanadas, Iz. I've just had a terrible week . . . and *weird*."

"You want to talk about it?" asked Isabel. She blew on her empanada and took a second bite, this time relishing the sweet, apple gooiness.

"No, that's okay," Elena Maria muttered.

Isabel rolled her eyes. "Come on, Elena. Don't tell me that you came into the room with a plate of deliciousness just because you thought I was hungry. Please . . . I'm your sister. I know you better than that!"

Elena broke into half a smile and rested her shoulder against Isabel's. "Fine. Long story short—Jimmy and I had another fight."

"How about long story long?"

Elena Maria shrugged. "Ugh, I don't even know where to begin. I guess it all started with the Snack Club."

Isabel raised her eyebrows. "Is that like the BSG of the ninth grade or something?"

Elena Maria shook her head. "No, no. Not at all. The Snack Club is this thing that the boys' indoor lacrosse team started. Ron Kylie—he's the captain—told all the guys on the team to get their girlfriends to show up at all the practices with snacks, for moral support or something."

"That's so lame," Isabel remarked. "As if girlfriends don't have their own things to do in the afternoon!"

"I know. You're so right, Izzie!"

"Hey, isn't Jimmy the co-captain?" Isabel inquired.

"Yes. Don't remind me. He definitely had something to do with the Club. And it gets worse," Elena Maria griped. "Ron and Jimmy made up the Snack Club's first rule . . . every practice they basically assign snack duty to two of the girl-friends—on game days, it's three girlfriends. We're supposed to bring enough food for the whole team *and* the coaches."

Isabel forced down the gulp of empanada that was in her mouth. "But that's practically impossible! Every one of those guys eats enough for twelve people!"

"I know. And get this—Jimmy volunteered *me* to be the president because I'm *soooo good* at cooking."

"Don't tell me you actually went along with this ridiculousness . . ." Isabel couldn't imagine that her fun-loving big sister would allow her life to revolve around Jimmy's lacrosse schedule and the monster appetites of a bunch of guys.

"Well, at first it was kind of fun. I mean, it was like a chance for me to test out my recipes. And everybody really liked what I brought. I did my famous four cheese pizza— the one with the basil and mozzarella."

"Mmm!" Isabel exclaimed.

"Then I made double chocolate cookies with cream cheese frosting."

"Ooh!" Isabel was practically drooling at the yummiliciousness of it all.

Elena Maria nodded. "I even brought them spicy chicken wings."

Isabel stopped her. "Not the wings! Elena, I can't believe you were making all that awesome food, and not sharing any with *me*! And by the way, who was paying for all of this?"

"Oh, all the guys chipped in, and the person who cooked didn't have to bring the napkins or anything. Then all of a sudden the basketball team wanted me to provide snacks for them, and Cammy was going to be the business manager, and we were going to do afternoon snacks for kids in detention— the whole thing got so out of control." Elena Maria sighed.

"I love cooking, but making food for everyone was taking up way too much time in the afternoons. And there was this great cooking class I wanted to take—Scott Madden told me about it. When I told Jimmy I signed up, he seemed excited for me—then he just kind of changed. He was like, 'Well, I hope you'll still have time to make snacks for the games.'"

Isabel's jaw nearly hit the floor.

"I know—you don't have to say a word." Elena Maria just shook her head like she couldn't even believe what she was saying. "Soooo anyway, I skipped the first class tonight, because it's the big game against Needham. And when I asked some of the other girls and guys to help, no one could. I spent the whole afternoon rolling empanada dough. These were the leftovers." Elena Maria's voice started to break and she swallowed back her tears. "Scott just called me to ask where I was. I—I felt so stupid telling him about the Snack Club. I told him I wasn't feeling well." Elena Maria unfolded the quilt from Isabel's bed and wrapped it around herself. "It's not even a lie, Iz. I feel awful . . . just awful."

Isabel rubbed her sister's back. "Do you feel awful 'cause Jimmy's taking advantage of you . . . or awful because you secretly have a crush on Scott?"

Elena Maria sat up with a start. "First of all, Jimmy's not really taking advantage of me. I wanted to do Snack Club, and I totally love it when people love my food. Everyone on the team and the other girls think I am like a famous chef already. Kyla Perkins told me my food was so good I should have my own TV show. And everybody, even goofy Tony Grimsby, says thank you . . . it's just that it's way too much. I mean I have schoolwork to do, and now I'm too tired."

Isabel bit her lip as Elena Maria went on. "Second of all, I *do not* have a crush on Scott. He's my friend. We have a lot in common. Girls *are* allowed to be just friends with guys, you know."

"Yeah . . . I know. Um, so other than the Snack Club, are things okay between you and Jimmy?"

Elena Maria nodded, then slowly the nod transformed into a head shake. "Actually, to tell you the truth, I don't think I really like Jimmy. He never calls me when he says he's going to. A few weeks ago he promised me that he'd take me out for dinner, then he made me meet him at Village Fare Pizza. When I got there he was waiting outside with three of his friends. And they all just talked about sports all night."

Isabel gaped. "No way."

"Way. And it gets worse. He said he left his wallet at home."

"Noooo *waaaaay!*" Isabel cried.

"Yup. And . . . so did his friends. Jimmy hasn't even paid me back yet, even after one of his friends who did pay me back got on his case."

Isabel jumped off the bed and twirled around. "Elena Maria, does the word 'user/loser' mean anything to you? Where is your brain, chica?"

"I just got so caught up with everybody telling me that I was the greatest cook . . . then everything got so messed up. And Jimmy was so cute and popular. And Jimmy just doesn't like Scott, and I have more fun hanging out with Scott, because he's funny and he really is a great cook. I mean, I couldn't tell Scott this, because I have my pride and all, but Scott's chili is better than mine. And anyway . . . ." Elena Maria paused. "I just don't want a boyfriend right now," she admitted.

"Uh-huh," Isabel said. "That makes sense considering that Jimmy is such a crummy boyfriend. It's like you need to take a breather."

"Exactly," her sister agreed. "I mean, Scott's awesome. He's a nice kid, he's . . . my friend. I love hanging out with him. We have so many things in common besides food. And he even said he would teach me to snowboard. Something Jimmy said he would do and never did."

Isabel smiled mischievously. "Loooove for Scott?"

Elena Maria lightly threw a pillow at her sister. "*No.* You know what I mean." She sighed. "I've been with Jimmy for a few months now, Iz. Maybe that's just how things get after a while. The whole boyfriend thing loses its . . . sparkle. Or something."

"Well, if you want my advice I'd take a little break from Jimmy, the user/loser," Isabel suggested, "'cause it sounds to me like your real dreamboat is waiting in the wings . . . or in the kitchen!"

Elena Maria blew her nose into a tissue and laughed. Charlotte made up a word for that: sniggle. Isabel thought that was perfect. "You know, Izzie, I promise you, Jimmy and I are finito!"

"Maybe I can have a chat with the BSG and see if Avery knows anything about Scott?" Isabel offered.

"Please, Iz, this isn't second grade! If something's going on between me and Scott—*which it isn't*—I want to figure it out myself," Elena Maria said decidedly.

Isabel flipped open her cartoon notebook. "Fine. Listen, I have a deadline coming up, so I have to start working on my cartoon . . ."

Elena Maria stood, stretched, and muttered, "I should get started on my homework too." She started towards the door, but froze halfway there. "Actually, Izzy . . . on the off chance that Avery *does* mention something about Scott . . . well, you can let me know."

"Got it." Isabel smirked. She threw her pillow at Elena Maria and added, "Sorry—I owed you one."

"Ouch!" Elena Maria laughed. "Thanks, sis. I needed that!"

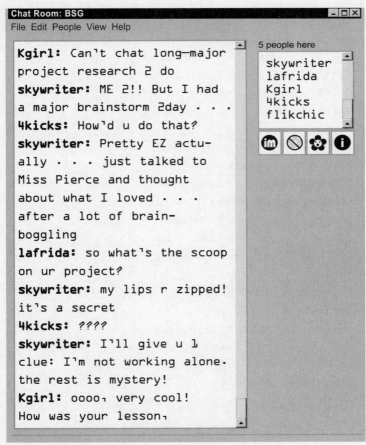

Maevalicious?

flikchic: fine.

Kgirl: JUST fine??? With Matt the Adorable?

flikchic: yeah.

4kicks: I have news. Cupid has struck the Madden household . . .

skywriter: Not you, Ave.

4kicks: hah! That's a good one . . . no . . . had a little chat with Scott 2nite

Kgirl: lemme guess . . . EM?

4kicks: Obvi. He's like a puppy. I tried to help, but I'm not that good with lovey-dovey stuff

lafrida: that's sooo funny! EM came to me 4 advice 2! It sounds like she is unhappy w/J . . . but she said that she and Scott are "just friends."

skywriter: That's called *denial*.

4kicks: I thought de-nile was a river in Egypt

Kgirl: har har har . . .

skywriter: don't you see!

5 people here

skywriter
lafrida
Kgirl
4kicks
flikchic

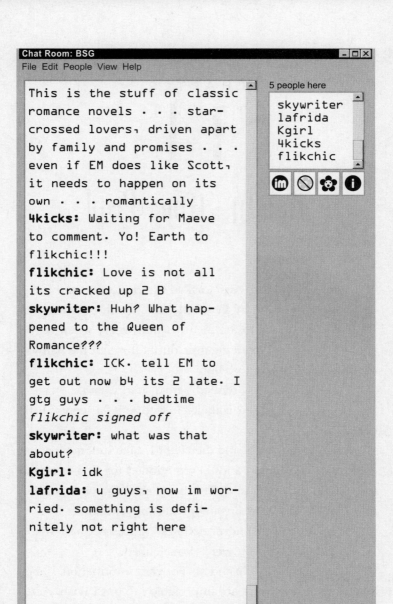

Chat Room: BSG

File Edit People View Help

This is the stuff of classic romance novels . . . star-crossed lovers, driven apart by family and promises . . . even if EM does like Scott, it needs to happen on its own . . . romantically

4kicks: Waiting for Maeve to comment. Yo! Earth to flikchic!!!

flikchic: Love is not all its cracked up 2 B

skywriter: Huh? What happened to the Queen of Romance???

flikchic: ICK. tell EM to get out now b4 its 2 late. I gtg guys . . . bedtime

flikchic signed off

skywriter: what was that about?

Kgirl: idk

lafrida: u guys, now im worried. something is definitely not right here

5 people here

skywriter
lafrida
Kgirl
4kicks
flikchic

14

Ready, Aim, Pop!

W hat's in the bag, Ave?" asked Charlotte. She and Isabel were standing by Charlotte's locker, discussing their contributions to the Sentinel that week, when they'd spotted Avery hauling a gigantic duffel through the hallway of Abigail Adams Junior High.

"You'll see," Avery replied with a snarky smirk.

"Come on," urged Isabel. "Just give us a teensy little clue."

Avery looked right and then left to make sure none of her enemies was listening and then motioned for Charlotte and Isabel to huddle in closer. "This bag," she began in a soft but important voice, "contains my greatest invention yet."

"A soccer ball that never deflates?" guessed Charlotte.

"A hair ribbon destroyer?" Isabel joked.

Avery groaned. "No and no. For your information, Isabel, hair ribbon destroyers are impossible . . . but I wish. Actually, it's five pounds of original, homemade Avery Madden chewing gum. It's stickier, tastier, and way better for you

than that Tru Blu stuff Kiki's been giving out. Check. It. Out."
She reached into her duffel and produced a small drawstring
bag. "Contained in this bio bag is the best gum you've ever
tasted!" she announced, and then dramatically pulled out a
long roll of gum with indentations along it.

"That's gum?" Isabel asked suspiciously, staring at the
gum roll in Avery's hand.

"I'm not chewing that!" Charlotte said decidedly. "It
looks kind of sketchy, Ave."

Avery rolled her eyes. "You guys, it's *supposed* to look
that way—the design cuts down on wasted wrappers, which
saves garbage *and* the manufacturing of all that paper, which
takes tons of water. And it comes in its own totally, completely biodegradable bag. This gum, my friends, is my way
to help save the planet—and I think it's pretty ingenious, if I
do say so myself. See?" She broke off a piece of the gum roll
and held it out. "Come on, Char—you trust me, right? Izzy?
Try a piece?"

Isabel grimaced and shook her head.

Avery gave a frustrated sigh. "Ugh. I expect more from
my BSG. You girls are *chickens*."

"Hey!" cried Isabel. "I resent that." She grabbed the
gum from Avery's outstretched hand, broke off a piece, and
stuffed it in her mouth. Gradually her skeptical scowl became
a broad grin. "Hey, Char, you gotta try this stuff. Wriff riff
rerry grrrd."

"What?" asked Charlotte.

Isabel folded the gum under her tongue and repeated, "I
said, this is really good. It tastes like berries but . . . you know
. . . tangy like!"

Avery was glowing. "Yeah? Nice! It took me eight hours last night to get the recipe right."

"Eight hours?" Charlotte balked. "You must have gotten like, no sleep!"

"Don't need sleep," Avery said, slapping her bag. "Got sugar! Pure cane sugar, actually."

"Hey, girls. What's in the giant duffel?" asked Katani. She strode over with an uncharacteristically serious-looking Maeve by her side.

"Well . . . so far, Avery made enough gum to last till 2012, and she's eaten enough sugar to keep her awake till next Thursday," Isabel explained.

"What's with all the gum?" asked Maeve.

"It's part of my master plan to take over the world . . . one gum wad at a time . . . wah, hah, hah!" Avery did her fake evil laugh.

"No, seriously," said Katani. "What's going on?"

"Wellllll . . . my master plan has four points of genius. One, the packaging for this gum is biodegradable, so when you are done enjoying its record-breaking awesomeness, you don't have to worry about it filling dumps for all eternity. And it comes in this nifty roll, which cuts down on even more packaging. It's like buying juice in a big bottle instead of a lot of little boxes—way better for the environment. Tru Blu Goo comes with every little piece wrapped up in its own paper wrapper! So not enviro-friendly.

"Two, this gum, *Avery Madden Gum*, is all natural. None of that nasty artificial sweetener stuff. I mean, 'aspartame'? Who even knows what that is? Three! Big gum factories like the one Kiki's dad is promoting use an artificial gum base that comes from petroleum. It's basically all wax and rubber and other chemically things . . . talk about ewwww. *My* gum gets most of it its sticky-wicky-deliciousness from chicle."

"Uh, what's that?" Isabel asked a little nervously, shifting the huge wad of Avery's gum to one side of her mouth so she could talk.

"Tree sap!" Avery exclaimed with a huge grin. Isabel looked pale. "But it's totally okay for you to chew it, Iz," Avery reassured her quickly. "It comes from these trees called sapodillas that grow in Central America. Like in the rain forest."

Isabel was looking less convinced by the second, so world-traveler and history buff Charlotte jumped in. "I've heard of that. I think I read somewhere that the Mayans used to chew chicle," she told Isabel encouragingly.

"Yep!" Avery agreed. "And that's not even the best part about chicle. Using it helps save the rain forest, because people harvest the sap from the trees over and over again. It doesn't hurt the trees at all and it gives people a good reason to not cut them down. And we need those rain forests, because more than a third of the species in the whole world live there, and all those trees and crazy-looking, giant plants absorb tons of carbon dioxide!"

"Ooo, Ife been weading abowt cawbon dioxide!" Isabel exclaimed. When the girls turned to her with confused looks, she tucked her huge wad of gum into her cheek and tried again. "Sorry! I said, I've been reading about carbon dioxide. It's one of those greenhouse gases, right? When there's too much of it in the atmosphere it can make the weather go crazy all over the world."

"Ding ding ding! Five enviro points for Isabel!" Avery shouted. "*And* using chicle helps the rain forest economy," she gushed, looking directly at Katani, "because it supports the people who live there and harvest the chicle."

"How do you know?" demanded Katani, still touchy from the conversation about the gum factory and the economy the day before.

"Hours of research, dude," Avery answered, pulling out a thick packet of papers from her backpack. "And I talked to the people at Glee Gum. But the third point of my master plan is the best of them all." Avery rubbed her hands together in what she hoped was a menacing way. "My gum is so much better than Kiki Underwood's that no one is going to care or even want that super yuuugly Tru Blu stuff. That is, once they try my masterpiece." Avery grinned at everyone.

"And just how do you plan on doing that?" asked Katani doubtfully. "Not that I'm on her side or anything, but it seems like Kiki's gum is pretty popular. All the kids at AAJH have been rocking bright blue tongue . . . if you haven't noticed."

Avery casually waved her hand. "Just watch. Hey, Nick!"

Nick Montoya jogged over to the BSG. "Hey, guys . . . hey, Charlotte."

"Hi," Charlotte said softly. Whenever Nick Montoya came around her knees turned to pudding. "Did you get my e-mail?"

The girls glanced at each other with raised eyebrows, but Maeve looked away. Usually seeing puppy love like Nick and Charlotte's made Maeve feel all warm and fuzzy inside. Today, however, it made her feel like bursting into tears and running into a bathroom stall. It didn't help that once—even though it was a while ago—Nick Montoya had been her crush project. But after one disastrous date, it was clear to Maeve and the rest of the BSG that Nick Montoya had eyes only for Charlotte.

"I was just gonna say!" Nick exclaimed to Charlotte. "I think it's an awesome idea. I just ran into Chelsea outside, and—"

"Shhhh!" Charlotte shushed him, tilting her head toward the rest of the BSG.

"Oh, right, top secret!" Nick answered, dropping his voice. "I mean, uh, I did *not* just run into Chelsea outside, and she definitely did *not* just tell me that she's totally on board."

Everyone, including Charlotte, had to grin. "I guess now we know who your partners-in-science-fair-crime are," Avery teased.

"That's great that she, uh, *didn't* say that," Charlotte laughingly told Nick. "Now, I say we talk to Ms. R after class and get her okay . . ."

"And then we can meet at the bakery today after school," Nick said, finishing Charlotte's sentence, almost as if the two shared one brain.

Avery rolled her eyes and mouthed, "True Love," even managing to right Maeve's perma-frown into a smile. "Listen, Nick, as much as we'd all like to hear about you and Char's secret meet-up-ez-vous—"

"Don't you mean *rendezvous*?" asked Charlotte, who was not only a word nerd, but had lived in Paris.

"Whatever," Avery went on. "The thing is, Nick, I called you over here for a reason."

"Oh, yeah? What?"

"I was wondering if you wanted to try a piece of my homemade gum." Avery broke off another section from the gum roll and extended her hand with the gum resting in her palm.

Nick leaned in. "Dude. That looks totally sketchy. I mean, *totally.*"

"That's just what I said!" Charlotte cried.

"It's actually weewy good," Isabel uttered between chews. "But I can't get it to make a bubble . . ." She made a funny face as she shifted the gum all around in her mouth, trying to blow a bubble.

"That's because it's *not* bubble gum, Iz," Avery told her. "It's *chewing* gum. You know what makes the bubbles in bubble gum? Elastic. And there's no *way* I am putting that in my gum! It's supposed to be natural, remember?" She shook her hand holding the gumball in front of Nick's nose. "So . . . Nick . . . whadaya say?"

He gritted his teeth and shook his head.

"Watch this," Avery whispered to Katani. Then she declared loudly to Nick, "I *dare* you."

Now Nick looked intrigued. "What'll you give me?"

Avery squinted and said in her most serious voice, "Respect."

Nick nodded. "Deal." And with that he took the gum and popped it in his mouth. "Hey! This is *rad*! You don't even miss the bubbles . . . I mean the elastic . . . whatever. Yo, Dillon, Yurtmeister . . . get over here." Dillon Johnson and Henry Yurt ran over to join the group. "You've got to try the Ave's gum, dudes. Avery, set 'em up with some of that."

Avery distributed the gum to the boys, who both gave her two thumbs way up. Soon, Avery had kids coming up to her in twos and threes shouting, "Gum! Gum!" Before the first bell rang, half the stock in her duffel bag was gone. As the girls hustled off to class, Avery turned to her friends and snickered, "You see that?"

Confident that her gum would soon be the AAJH gum of choice, Avery stopped in front of her locker to store the rest. Her face turned purple when she grabbed her locker handle. Blue stickiness smushed through her fingers. She narrowed her eyes and whispered, "Let the games begin!"

Math Boy Strikes Again

"Hello! We're home!" Katani hollered. She and Kelley walked into the hallway and were greeted by silence. "Hey! Anybody here? I said we're home!" shouted Katani.

Kelley put her bag down and carefully hung up her yellow raincoat on its proper hook. "This is *peculiar*." Peculiar had been her word of the day. She knew it meant weird and had used it five times on their walk home. The only near-disaster was when she asked a man in a cowboy hat, "Why are you wearing a peculiar hat?" Katani didn't think the cowboy hat man had appreciated that.

"Hey, girls, how was school?" Patrice appeared in the hallway sucking down one of her banana soy milkshakes. She loved to make them after especially exhausting basketball practices.

"It was . . . okay. A little out of control," Katani mumbled.

"It was *peculiar*," Kelley pronounced. "Too much gum. There was gum everywhere. It wasn't normal." She laughed.

"What?" Patrice raised her eyebrows and collapsed in the easy chair in the den off the hallway. "I need to know more."

"Kids can be really immature," Katani muttered. "Kiki Underwood is trying to be the Gum Queen of Massachusetts— as if being a Queen of Mean isn't enough."

"You guys still call those girls that? Speaking of immature," Patrice teased. She just loved to get under Katani's skin.

"Whatever, Patrice. Besides, some gremlin kids are taking her silly blue gum and sticking it on stuff everywhere. Why anyone could think that's funny is beyond me. Then Avery made this gum at home that she said was better than Kiki's and brought it to school today. By lunch, all you could hear at Abigail Adams was chewing and popping. And of course some doodle-brains lack the *decency* to throw their completely repulsive, used gum in the trashcan. Ugh. Seventh grade can be such a zoo. Now there's gum *everywhere*. Doorknobs . . . chairs . . . desks . . . it's really disgusting. Like totally *out of control*. I think I'm going to have to talk to Grandma about this."

"Out of control," echoed Kelley. "Totally out of control . . . and very peculiar."

Patrice got up and peered out the window that overlooked the garage. "Are you even listening?" Katani challenged.

"What? Oh, forgive me if I'm not completely fascinated by your, um, gum story. I'm more interested in the junior-hottie situation going down in the garage."

"What junior hottie situation?"

Patrice shrugged. "I don't know. About an hour ago some

kid came over and wanted to talk to Dad. I've never seen him before, but he looks like he's about your age. He had this crazy messy 'fro and freckles, and he was wearing these awesome shades."

Katani shot over to the window and squeezed next to Patrice. There in her very own garage, on her very own property, chatting with her very own *dad*, was the one and only *Reggie DeWitt*. "I'll see about that . . . ," she grumbled as she stormed out of the house.

"Where are you going, Katani?" Kelley called after her. "She's in a very peculiar mood!" she remarked to Patrice.

Patrice smiled. "Very peculiar indeed."

"Just what do you think you're doing, Reggie?" Katani demanded, marching into the garage with her arms crossed tensely across her chest.

"Yo yo, Kgirl, 'sup holmes?" Reggie greeted her.

Katani clenched her fists. She'd had about enough of the new Reggie. She turned to her father. "Dad, what's going on here?"

Mr. Summers looked confused. "Well, young Reggie here expressed a keen interest in learning the nuts and bolts of—"

"*Ahem*," Reggie coughed.

"Oh, right. No revealing the top-secret science project." Mr. Summers chuckled.

Katani looked appalled. "How do you two even *know* each other?"

Reggie spoke up, sounding slightly more like his normal self. "I'm a big fan of your father's work. He was the one who did the wiring for the new movie theater downtown. I wanted to work with the best, so I called the theater and they referred me to Mr. Summers . . . your dad, I mean."

"Ever since I got my big commission for the new gum factory, I've been able to cut out a lot of my smaller jobs to spend more time at home. And after all," her dad continued bashfully, "he is my only electricity fan to date. But don't worry, scout—I'll still have plenty of time to give you a hand with your project, too. You don't mind, do you?"

Katani opened her mouth, ready to yell that she *did* mind, that she couldn't stand Reggie DeWitt, and she wanted nothing more than for him to march his baggy jeans and his phony personality out of her garage, off of her property, and *away from her dad*. But instead, she bit her lip and uttered with all the strength she could possibly muster, "No. No problem. I'm gonna go start my homework." She ran over and kissed her dad on the cheek. "Love you, Dad."

"Love you, too, princess."

Katani did her most confident, model walk—she had walked the runway once in New York—right out of the garage.

"Hey, Katani!" Reggie called after her.

She froze and slowly turned around.

"You forgot your scarf in the science room yesterday." Reggie waved the yellow silk in the air.

Katani hated feeling forgetful or anything less than her usual pulled-together self, so it didn't help that she had to walk all the way back across the garage to retrieve the scarf. Plus, her father noted, "That's very nice of you, Reggie."

"So . . . ," Patrice probed when she returned. "What's the deal with McCutie?"

"You can't be serious," Katani said, disgusted. "Reggie DeWitt is so . . . so . . . annoying."

Patrice threw back her head and began to laugh hysterically.

"What?" Katani cried. "What's so funny?"

"Oh . . . nothing."

Katani squinted. "You can't do that. You have to tell me. What?"

Patrice wiped a laughter tear out of the corner of her eye. "It's just either you have like, a major crush on that kid, or Kelley's totally right . . . you *are* peculiar!"

CHAPTER

15

Dream-Crush Cowboy

Maeve was being haunted, not by a ghost, but by the image of Bailey. Wherever she went, whatever she did, she saw Matt's girlfriend. She couldn't even enjoy wearing her favorite pink ensembles, because all she could think about was Matt telling her, "I really couldn't care less about clothes."

Maeve marched around her bedroom, glaring at her reflection in her dresser mirror. "What does *she* have that I don't have?" Maeve wondered aloud. Matt had said that Bailey was thoughtful. "I'm thoughtful too," Maeve attested, pushing away the nagging guilt that she'd behaved less than thoughtfully on a number of occasions that week.

After an hour of pacing and serious contemplation, Maeve finally arrived at the conclusion that there was only one reasonable explanation for Matt choosing Bailey over her, and that was that Bailey was a sophisticated woman while she, Maeve Kaplan-Taylor, was . . . not.

She wondered what she would look like when she was

Bailey's age. Maeve studied her face in the mirror and suddenly had an idea. She ran into Ms. Kaplan's room and returned with her mother's charcoal-colored eye liner and max-volume mascara. Maeve had a little makeup collection of her own, but it had been decided by the higher powers (her parents) that she was much too young for eyeliner and mascara.

With all the precision she could muster, Maeve very carefully outlined her big, blue eyes and combed the gooey black mascara through her long lashes. "Wow!" she breathed as she stared, pleased, at the result. "Hello, Mr. Agent. I'd love to go to LA and star in your zabillion dollar movie. Of course, I have to finish up my important scientific research on the importance of organically grown daffodils. Can you wait for me?" She dusted her cheeks with blush, smeared on dark red lipstick, and tied back her hair with a big silver clip.

Maeve waltzed over to her big teddy bear sitting on the chair in the corner of her room. "Why, hello, Caleb. Why of course I'll be going to Bedazzle's after the Golden Globes. You'd like to go with me? Well, D-Cap did ask me first, but I'm still free for the Oscars if you'd like to—" Maeve stopped suddenly as she heard a quiet giggling noise coming from the hallway.

She quickly dashed over to the door and opened it, knocking over Sam, who'd been perched outside with his eye glued to her keyhole. "*Ow*! Maeve!"

"*Sam*! Were you *spying* on me?" she demanded. "*Mom! Sam's teasing me again!*"

"Was not! *Mom, Maeve is lying to you!*"

Maeve knew there really was no worse sound than a mother thudding down the hall to deal with her screaming children. Maeve and Sam were both trembling as they real-ized their mistake. "What is going on here? Sam, it's nine o'clock. Why aren't you in bed?"

Ooo, two points for me! Maeve cheered silently. Sam was up past his bedtime.

"Um . . . um . . . Maeve stole your makeup and woke me up."

"Stop it, Sam!" Maeve shrieked, batting her brother's hands away as he grabbed the shimmery scarf she had draped over her shoulders. Her brother was being so annoying that Maeve wanted to scream.

"And Maeve," Ms. Kaplan put her hands on her hips, "what's going on with this atrocious stage makeup look?"

"You mean I look like I belong onstage?" asked Maeve hopefully.

"No, dear. It's not a compliment. You have got on way *waaaay* too much makeup."

"Oh." Maeve felt a little sorry for herself, but in one second had recollected her bearings and remembered, "But Mom, Sam was *spying* on me!"

Ms. Kaplan raised her arms in the air and cried, "*Enough!* Sam, in bed *now*. And by the way, young man, if you don't stop torturing your sister, you're grounded for the whole month . . . and I mean it! Maeve," Ms. Kaplan opened the door to Maeve's bedroom and ushered her inside, "young lady, you're coming with me."

Maeve wasn't sure if this was a good thing or a bad thing, but she followed her mother into the room. Ms. Kaplan sat on the bed and motioned for Maeve to do the same. "Okay. So what's wrong, sweetie?"

"Nothing. Why?"

Ms. Kaplan squinted. "You've been moping around this house for days. Honestly, you made more noise before you could even talk, Maeve. Now be honest with me. Is it school . . . friends . . . parties? Are you sneaking out of here to go to a party?"

Maeve furiously shook her head. "No! No way, Mom."

"Well, I don't see any other explanation for this," she waved her hand in front of Maeve's overly decorated face and continued, "unless . . . ,"

"Unless, what?"

Ms. Kaplan stroked her daughter's face and asked softly, "Are you in love?"

Maeve's lower lip began to tremble. "I'm not in love," she squeaked, and at that moment she couldn't hold it in anymore and burst into tears. "I'm—I'm *completely heartbroken*!" Maeve began to sob and collapsed into her mother's lap.

Ms. Kaplan reached out and patted Maeve's back. "Shh . . . shh . . . there, there, sweetie. I feel terrible . . . I didn't even know you had a boyfriend."

Maeve sat up and blubbered, "That's 'cause I never did!" Then she threw herself back down.

"You want to talk about it?" asked Ms. Kaplan.

"No," Maeve heaved. "Well, maybe. You see, there's this guy. And he's a little bit older . . . actually quite a bit older than me. And I thought he really liked me, you know? 'Cause he was always extra nice to me, and he even had this nickname for me—Mix-Master-Curl. Isn't that cute?"

"This guy," began Ms. Kaplan, "he wouldn't happen to be a certain"—she raised an eyebrow—"tutor?"

Maeve breathed a deep sigh. "Yes."

"So all this makeup and"—Maeve's mother looked at the discarded shimmery scarf on the floor—". . . stuff. This was just to look older?"

Maeve nodded. "Matt told me that he—he—he—" Her voice started to quake and then she wailed, "has a"—*sniff, sniff*—"*girlfriend.*" Maeve cried as her mother stroked her back. "It's this college girl . . . she's totally unglamorous and like, way into science, and he thinks she just s-s-super a-awesome and I'm j-just s-s-so sad!"

Maeve's mother leaned over and plucked a tissue out of Maeve's pink, fuzzy tissue box. "Here, honey. You got a little schmutz." She directed Maeve to her reflection in the mirror, and Maeve saw that all the eyeliner and mascara that she'd so tenderly applied was now running down her cheeks in two thick, black streaks.

Maeve screamed, "Aaah! I look horrible! No wonder Matt doesn't like me. . . . *I'm a hideous mess!*"

Ms. Kaplan had to stifle a small giggle. Even in her daughter's hour of despair, she still managed to transform the scene into something fit for the silver screen.

"To think," Maeve moaned as she wiped the black gunk off her face, "I was so"—*sniff, sniff*—"sure he was my"—*sniff, sniff*—"*soul mate!*"

"Maeve, did I ever tell you about my first crush?" asked Ms. Kaplan in a soft voice.

"You mean Dad?" asked Maeve. Even though her parents were separated, Maeve knew that when they got married they were very much in love.

Ms. Kaplan blushed and replied, "No, *before* your father.

You know, when I was a girl, I was a lot like you in many ways. I remember—I must've been about eleven—and I was completely head over heels for Derek Duncan . . . the most handsome cowboy in the world."

Maeve's eye's widened. "Whoa . . . *you knew a cowboy?*" she gasped.

Ms. Kaplan laughed. "Well no, not personally. He was actually the star of my favorite Western soap opera, *Trouble Canyon*. I knew every episode by heart. Every Tuesday I'd run all the way home from school to watch Derek Duncan steal fair maidens' hearts and rustle up the bad guys in the saloon . . . oh and you should have seen him ride his black stallion, Trusty Rusty. Now *that* was television."

"Trusty Rusty?" Maeve raised an eyebrow. "*Really,* Mom!"

Ms. Kaplan shrugged. "All right, maybe it was a little cheesy. But at the time, Derek Duncan meant everything to me. I remember, I used to write Carol Gwendolyn Duncan and Mrs. Carol Gwendolyn Duncan on my notebook over and over again. Gosh, I can only imagine what my teachers thought."

"But Mom, Gwendolyn's not even your middle name!" Maeve pointed out.

"I know, but when I was eleven, I wished it were Gwendolyn. Still do, to be honest with you. Anyway, one day the cover of *Soap Opera Soup*—that was my favorite magazine— announced that Derek Duncan had in *real life* married his costar Serena Fallon. I was devastated . . . totally, completely heartbroken. I played sick from school for three days and told my mom I had a terrible cold, because my eyes were so red and puffy. Really I'd been crying nonstop. Finally my mom realized what was going on. We had a big sit-down and she told me that Derek Duncan was a dream-crush, the kind you can always have in your dreams or your imagination as a . . . let's say . . . an example of what you might eventually be looking for. I think, Maeve, that a dream-crush would be the perfect way to describe Matt for you. He's a very nice boy . . . the kind you might like someday . . . when you're much older."

"You know what, Mom?" said Maeve, sniffling. "I think you might be right. I sort of thought that even if Matt and I didn't, like, you know, date *now* he'd wait for me to get a little bit older and *then* we'd date. But now that I think about it, Matt gets way more excited about math and science than I could ever be. I mean, even *I'm* not that good of an actress— ya know what I mean?"

Ms. Kaplan laughed. "Different strokes for different folks."

"Bailey really likes science." Maeve sniffled. "She helped me start my science project this weekend."

"And Bailey is Matt's . . . ,"

"Girlfriend," they both said at once. And then mother and daughter burst out laughing. Maeve couldn't believe how much better a little giggling could make her feel.

"Oh, Maeve, it's okay to feel heartbroken. It's just another part of growing up."

Maeve smiled. "I guess I've been doing a lot of that lately."

Ms. Kaplan nodded. "Uh-huh. And look at it this way— it's a lot easier to get over a dream-crush. Trust me, I have complete faith that you will have no problemo when it comes to romance."

Maeve's eyes perked up. "Really?"

"Absolutely!" Ms. Kaplan assured and with a wink added, "As long as you find someone *else* to do your makeup. Now," she glanced at the door, "I was going to wait for a special occasion to give these to you, but I think your first heartbreak is as good a time as any. I'll be right back." She turned to leave and then, looking back, added, "And Maeve . . . you really are growing up."

"Mom?"

"Yes, sweetheart?"

"Matt's girlfriend Bailey . . ." Maeve put her hand to her heart and let out a deep breath at hearing her own voice speak the name "Bailey."

"Bailey what, honey?" Her mother looked down at her watch.

"Bailey thinks I have the soul of a botanist."

"Honey." Her mother grinned. "You have only just begun to discover your talents."

When her mother was gone, Maeve flopped back on her fluffy pink pillows and stared at the ceiling for a minute, taking a moment to imagine herself as a famous (and famously glamorous) botanist, sashaying down rows of magnificent blooms in a long, pink gown. Then she sighed, sat up, and flipped open her laptop. Time to get down to plant business.

File Edit People View Help

flikchic: hey Bailey. do u have time to talk ab my project right now?

GreenThumbelina: you got it, Maeve. what's up?

flikchic: so I know I'm testing ur fertilizer on daffodils . . . but I forgot 2 write down that other name 4 daffodils . . . like the sciency 1 . . .

GreenThumbelina: ur thinking "narcissus." named after a Greek god who fell in love w/ his own reflection—so u know they're beautiful!

flikchic: lol

GreenThumbelina: and I'm so excited—I know the perfect variety for u! They're called Paperwhites and they have tons of little white blooms, all clumped together like a sunburst. spectacular!

flikchic: sounds so pretty!

GreenThumbelina: ur gonna luv them, I just know it. we have some bulbs in the lab

2 people here

flikchic
Greenthum-
belina

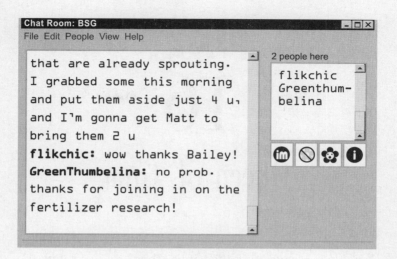

Chat Room: BSG

File Edit People View Help

that are already sprouting.
I grabbed some this morning
and put them aside just 4 u,
and I'm gonna get Matt to
bring them 2 u

flikchic: wow thanks Bailey!
GreenThumbelina: no prob.
thanks for joining in on the
fertilizer research!

2 people here

flikchic
Greenthum-
belina

When Maeve finally closed her eyes that evening, it wasn't Matt she dreamt of. Rather, it was large, pink peonies, and daffodils . . . sunny yellow and glorious white . . . all fertilized with Maeve's own Pinkalicious, all-organic fertilizer!

16

Queen of Gum

W hen Maeve swooshed into school the next day, the crowd literally parted in two. Maeve smiled at her gathering fans, knowing that she was truly a sight to behold. She'd transformed her tight red ringlets into sleek waves. She was wearing a stretchy white V-neck T-shirt, her enormous, glam-tastic movie star sunglasses, and a pair of designer jeans. Well . . . "designer" in so far as the one and only Katani Summers had embellished Maeve's favorite flares with magenta embroidered roses and sparkling rhinestones. But the best part of all was what was on her feet: pink boots, the very pair she'd seen at the mall with her mother a few weeks before. She couldn't believe her mom had remembered and had gone to the trouble and expense of going back to buy them for her.

Before she'd left for school, her mother had given her a few pointers on how to wear mascara. "At your age and with your complexion," Ms. Kaplan advised, "clear mascara is the way to go. Black is dramatic, but on a redhead everyone will know it's not natural." She let Maeve have her spare clear mascara, and Maeve couldn't believe how stunning her lush lashes looked. Sometimes mothers could be so sweet!

Maeve pretended not to notice when Dillon, Nick, and the Trentini twins gaped at her as she strutted into Ms. R's homeroom.

"*Muy caliente!*" Isabel gasped.

Maeve giggled. "*Gracias, mi amiga.*"

Katani gave her an approving nod. "You look fierce, girl!" Maeve couldn't help blushing. Some days her overly pink mood and 'tude could be a little bit much—as Katani often reminded her—but today she was sure she'd gotten it down just right!

"Wow," Charlotte remarked. "You seemed so sad these past few days and now, well, *look at you*. What happened?"

Maeve shrugged. "Let's just say the Queen of Romance is back and better than ever!"

"Good," Isabel said, wrapping her arm around Maeve's shoulders, "because we can't do this whole Scott/Elena Maria matchmaking thing without you!"

"Ooh, speaking of . . ." Charlotte began, "Dad gave me the thumbs up for an official BSG sleepover in the Tower on Saturday. Are you guys in?"

Maeve started clapping, as Katani and Isabel exclaimed, "Yeah!"

"Oh, look, it's BSG number five!" Maeve sang as Avery sprinted into the room just as the last bell rang. "Hey, Ave—sleepover at Char's this weekend!" Maeve informed her.

"Oh, yeah? Cool. Uuughhh!" Avery grunted as she hauled the garbage bag she was holding onto the chair of her desk.

"Don't tell me . . . ," Katani mumbled.

"Oh, yeah, you'd better believe it." Avery rubbed her hands together maniacally. "The biggest, baddest batch o' gum yet!" She reached in and came up with chunks of green. "Finally got the green coloring to work. I call it Green Tea Lime Fusion." She plopped a ball of gum in each of the BSG's hands.

"And just what are you planning on doing with all this?" Katani asked.

"Simple," answered Avery. "I am conducting a scientific experiment as we speak. The subjects are the students of Abigail Adams Junior High. Once people see that cutting down on packaging and making gum from natural materials isn't hard, tastes better, and helps save the rain forest, we might have a shot at stopping that factory. Can't you see it now—my recipe goes all over the world and nobody buys gum anymore, 'cause everybody can make it at home. That cuts out the packaging completely! But don't ask me for the recipes yet, loyal fans . . . I'm building suspense . . . everybody will have to wait until I release *those* on the night of the science fair."

"But, Avery, weren't you all, like, concerned about the greenhouse gases the factory will create?" Katani reminded her. "Did you do any research about that? Like how much CO_2 this *particular* factory will *actually* release into the atmosphere? And what makes you think everyone is going to like *your* gum so mu—"

Katani was interrupted by a sudden rush of kids crowding around Avery's desk with outstretched hands. "Avery! Avery! Over here! Avery! Toss me a piece, please!" The only ones to hang back were Anna and Joline, who looked quite sullen chewing their Tru Blu gum.

"Step right up! Step right up and get your gum! Save the planet!" Avery called, showering gum all around like she was riding a Mardi Gras float.

Charlotte glanced at Anna and Joline sulking in the corner and noted to Isabel, "I guess there's a new Queen of Gum around here!"

"Queen of Romance and Queen of Gum . . . I knew the BSG would be going places, I just didn't know it would be so soon!" Isabel giggled.

But Katani had a hard time rejoicing in Avery's gum success. *What if Avery's plan actually works?* she wondered. *If enough people rally against the new gum factory, then Dad might lose his contract. He'll have to go back to working a million little jobs, and he won't be at home nearly as much.*

As the kids shuffled out of homeroom and off to first period, Ms. Rodriguez pulled Avery aside. "I need to speak with you a minute, Avery . . . it's about your gum project."

Katani felt a pang of hope that maybe Ms. R was going to put a stop to all this crazy gum business.

"Great news, guys!" Avery chirped as she waltzed into science class. "Ms. R told me the science department approved 'a small grant' for me to make more gum and print out a recipe book. She said as a fellow environmental advocate she really admires my initiative!"

Katani, who was sitting on a stool across from Avery at the BSG's favorite lab table, gasped. "Wait a minute. *That's* what she had you stay after homeroom about?"

Avery beamed. "Uh-huh!"

"That's great!" Maeve gushed. Charlotte and Isabel nodded enthusiastically.

"Is something wrong, Katani?" Avery asked. Katani
wasn't great about keeping her feelings to herself and the
frown she was wearing was almost identical to the ones
Anna, Joline, and Kiki were sporting on the other side of
the room.

"Nope." Katani dove into her school bag and began rus-
tling around. The rest of the BSG looked at each other nervously, feeling the tension in the air. "Argh! Where is my
calculator!?" she growled. Katani leapt up and as she did, the
BSG stared in horror as a string of bright green gum stretched
from the back pocket of her chic camel-colored pants to the
chair.

"Uh, Katani . . ." Maeve hesitantly pointed at the trail.

"Ewwwww!" she shrieked picking the gum off the fabric.
"I am so, so sick of this stupid gum!" Katani marched away
to find a calculator.

"Whoa! What the heck is bugging the Kgirl?" Avery
asked. She wound her finger around her ear to show that she
thought Katani was cracking up.

"Shh, listen!" Isabel insisted. The BSG huddled around
the center of the table. "Katani called me last night. She's more
freaked out about this gum factory thing than we thought.
The deal is, she's really worried that Avery's gonna win the
gum war and put the factory out of business and her dad's
going to lose his commission."

"That's crazy!" Maeve exclaimed.

"*Shhh!*" the girls said at once.

"I mean," Maeve dropped to a whisper, "one kid can't stop a major factory from coming in. . . ."

Avery's face darkened. "Hey. Are you with the Green Machine or against it?"

"She's coming back guys. Shhh," Charlotte warned.

The girls retreated to their stools and immediately began studying their science books. Katani eyed her friends dubiously.

The girls all felt relieved when Mr. Moore started class. But for once, they wished he was conducting a lecture instead of a lab. A lab meant half work, half chat. And today, they could smell trouble brewing.

Charlotte took the wheel on the experiment—looking at strands of hair under a microscope. The instructions specified that the students do a comparative analysis of various hair types under the microscope: curly, straight, and three different colors. "We're so lucky we can cover all the hair types without even looking outside the BSG!" Charlotte pointed out.

"Here, take one of mine! Ouch!" Avery plucked a strand of her long, black hair.

"Maeve?" asked Charlotte with an outstretched hand.

"But my hair is perfectly styled today," Maeve objected. "This 'do took me aaaaages, you guys."

"But it says," Isabel leaned over and read from the assignment sheet, "one red hair."

"Cough it up, sister," Katani demanded.

"All right! What I do for science," Maeve grumbled as she yanked one of her hairs out.

"Uh-oh!" Avery interrupted. "We've got a bigger problem,

girls. Look!" She pointed at Mr. Moore, who was making a chart on the chalkboard for the class to fill in their collected data.

"He's got your green gum all over the back of his pants!" Maeve shouted.

"Keep it down, would ya?" Avery said, panicked. "If he finds out *my* gum is on his pants, I could lose everything!"

"Well, somebody's got to tell him. Look at my pants! This stuff stains like crazy," Katani objected. "You should have done better research, Avery."

"Oh, come on!" Avery groaned. "Since when do *you* care about Mr. Moore's clothing status?"

Katani narrowed her eyes and breathed, "You *know* I care about *everyone's* clothing status."

"She does love fashion," Charlotte offered.

The girls all turned and watched the gum shake back and forth from Mr. Moore's pants like a little green tail. There were giggles from around the room as other kids looked up and noticed. "This is too humiliating . . . Mr. Moore is a great teacher," Katani remarked. "I'm gonna tell him."

"No!" shrieked Avery. "I know what this is about, Katani. You're afraid that my gum project is going to take down the factory and your dad will lose his big commission, and now you're trying to sabotage me!"

"Avery!" Katani gasped. "I would never sabotage a friend. How could you even think that?" Katani folded her arms and for a second Maeve wondered if smoke was going to stream out of her nostrils.

Maeve took a deep breath and decided to step into the role of peacemaker. She had done it before for the girls, and she was happy to do it again. But as soon as she opened her mouth to give her famous let bygones be bygones speech, she realized someone else had stolen her lines!

"All right, everybody calm down!" Isabel insisted. "I can't believe that you guys are letting all this stuff about the gum factory blow up over this—a weird little gum tail on Mr. Moore's doofy pants."

Charlotte and Maeve let out a giggle, but Avery and Katani were still fuming.

"Hello! Warning! Don't you guys remember why we started this science fair thing?" Isabel insisted.

Maeve raised her hand "Ooh! I do! Pick me!"

Avery rolled her eyes. "To do our part to save the environment."

Katani nodded. "Agreed."

"And isn't part of saving the environment working together!?" Isabel asked. Now she was really rolling.

"Yes," mumbled Avery and Katani at the same time.

"I don't want your dad to lose his commission." Avery sighed. "I just really, *really* wanted to show the Queens of Mean that not everyone was part of their zombie consumer tribe . . . that kids do care about the environment."

Katani shrugged. "I know. It's just, things got so complicated. I want to help the environment too, obviously. But I also like having my dad home more."

"So this is a truce?" Charlotte asked.

"*Yes!*" the girls answered at once.

Avery had the girls put their all hands on top of one another. "Let's go, Green Machine!" she cried as they all lifted their hands to the ceiling.

As the girls finished up their lab, Mr. Moore walked over to their table. "Avery, I was wondering if I could have a word with you?"

"Suuuure . . . " Avery nervously replied, noticing out of the corner of her eye that Kiki and Anna were doubled over in laughter. She'd already stayed after class once today without getting in trouble—surely she couldn't get that lucky twice!

Mr. Moore went to his desk to grade papers as the students filtered out. When everyone had finally left, it was just him and Avery, and he didn't even look up.

"*Ahem,*" Avery coughed, but no response. "*Ach . . . AHEM!*" she tried again.

Mr. Moore looked up. "Ah, yeah. Avery. We have a little problem on our hands."

The image of Mr. Moore's pants and green gum flashed in Avery's mind. "Yes?"

Mr. Moore took off his glasses and said in a very serious tone, "It's about your gum."

Avery gulped. "Uh-huh . . ."

"Well, I first wanted to congratulate you on all the work you've done in developing your product. I think it's wonderful that you are thinking about the chemical content in commercial gum and concerned with producing environmentally-friendly products. And of course the science department was thrilled to see a student really take a cause in the community and make it her own."

"Uh, thank you," Avery answered nervously.

"That being said," Mr. Moore began.

Oh, no! Here it comes . . . the gum wars are out of control and now he's going to want me to kill my project.

"I was going over your project packet that was due yesterday. I see that you've done some good research on how trees are important to the environment because they absorb CO_2, but you're missing one piece of the puzzle in order to evaluate the total potential environment impact of the factory. Why don't you look into what the factory's carbon emissions will be?"

"Carbon emissions?" Avery repeated, vaguely remembering Betsy Fitzgerald saying something about that. And now that she thought of it, didn't Katani mention that term, too? "Is that like greenhouse gases and stuff? I know a little bit about that . . ."

"It is," Mr. Moore replied. "What do you know about the carbon cycle?"

"Uh . . . I know it's bad."

Mr. Moore shook his head. "Actually, the carbon cycle itself isn't a bad thing. It's a perfectly natural process for the Earth. Sort of like breathing. The ocean absorbs and releases carbon dioxide from the atmosphere, and plants take in and release carbon dioxide as they grow, which helps keep the whole system in balance. Things only get bad when more carbon dioxide is released into the atmosphere than the plants and the ocean can absorb. The carbon dioxide lets heat from the sun pass through it, but then it doesn't let the heat get back out. That extra heat can cause trouble for the climate of the whole Earth."

"How does that happen? How does extra carbon dioxide get up there?" Avery was captivated by what Mr. Moore was saying.

"Well, people create a lot of carbon dioxide when they burn fossil fuels for energy. So, for example, if this gum factory uses a lot of energy from fossil fuels, it could be responsible for sending a lot of extra carbon dioxide into the atmosphere. People call the carbon dioxide that's released the 'carbon emission,' and how much carbon dioxide the factory is responsible for is its 'carbon footprint.'" Mr. Moore paused and looked seriously at Avery. "Why don't you call their office and see if they have any information? Most companies have brochures they send out to local citizens."

"Okay," Avery breathed. She knew her fun with gum had been too good to be true. "Is that . . ." She paused. ". . . all, Mr. Moore?"

He looked up. "Yes, that's all. I'm sorry, Avery. It seems that we find ourselves in a rather sticky situation." He chuckled at his little joke and then went back to work.

Avery slung her bag over her shoulder and tried to swallow her smile as she sauntered out the door. *That was a close one!* she thought to herself. *And all this carbon stuff sounds more complicated than I thought.*

As she walked, or in Avery's case, practically skipped down the hall, visions of a huge, hairy carbon footprint caused her to laugh out loud. Unfortunately, QOM #1, Anna, was just coming out of the girl's room. When she saw Avery laughing she twirled her finger by the side of her head and rolled her eyes.

"Trying out for a cartoon series, Anna?" Avery quipped as she ran by. No QOM could get the better of her!

CHAPTER

17

That's What Friends Are For

"Okay, Charlotte. Indian, Chinese, or Thai?" asked Mr. Ramsey. He popped into Charlotte's bedroom with a handful of takeout menus.

Charlotte looked at her dad like he was crazy. "Dad, this is an official *BSG sleepover*, remember?"

Mr. Ramsey nodded. "Pizza. Gosh, I don't know why I even bother to ask anymore! You girls have pizza on the brain!" Marty yipped happily in the corner, jumped out of his bed, and ran around in a series of figure eights around Charlotte and her dad. Marty got just as excited for BSG sleepovers as Charlotte did, and he got extra excited for pizza.

Charlotte laughed at Marty's antics and scooped him up into a cuddle. "Just make sure there's no onions or garlic on the pizza, 'kay Dad?" Charlotte reminded him. "Looks like Marty wants to share, and those things can be poisonous for dogs!"

"I wouldn't forget, Char," her dad assured her. Just then the doorbell rang.

"Yikes!" Charlotte cried. "I can't believe it's five o'clock already! I still haven't cleaned up my science fair project from in the Tower. Can you get the door, Dad?"

Charlotte usually made a point of keeping her school-work very neat—particularly where sleepovers were concerned. She'd been working on her project all day with Nick and Chelsea Briggs. But when Chelsea left to go take pictures of a local crafts fair for the *Sentinel*, Charlotte and Nick had gotten caught up talking, laughing, and watching episodes of "Jungle Bloopers," their favorite nature exploration show, and she'd totally lost track of time. The truth was, she wished she could've hung out with Nick more.

When Charlotte raced upstairs to put away her supplies so the mess wouldn't give away what she and Nick and Chelsea were planning, she had no idea where to begin. "Roo-rooo!" Marty sang behind her. He skipped over to her palette of wet paint and showed off for Charlotte with one of his trademark rolls. He popped up and his normally grey and white patchy fur was covered in blue.

"Marty! You weren't supposed to come up here yet!" Charlotte groaned. "Daaad!"

"Hey, it's blue dog!" giggled Maeve. She stood in the doorway with Avery, Isabel, and Katani in the stairway behind her.

"Oh! You're here already!" Charlotte exclaimed, scooping Marty into her arms with a paint-smeared sheet. "Uhh ... can you guys hang out downstairs for a second? Just one little second!" As the BSG waited impatiently on the old, ladder-like stairs leading up the Tower, Charlotte went into overdrive mode, using her free hand—the one not cradling a wiggly dog, football-style—to drape more old sheets over everything she and Chelsea and Nick had been working on. She didn't want her super-secret project revealed until their big presentation at the science fair.

"Okay!" she called after a frantic minute. "You guys can come up now!" The rest of the BSG trooped into the room. "This is a first! Never in the history of BSG sleepovers have you all showed up at the same time. Usually . . ." Charlotte glanced at Maeve with a sly smile, ". . . at least one of you guys is running late."

"Sorry to disappoint you, Char," said Maeve, collapsing into the lime green swivel chair, "but today we had a romance emergency."

"Romance emergency?" Mr. Ramsey repeated, appearing at the top of the stairs. "Is that like when you choke on a heart-shaped chocolate? Ooh, or cut your finger on a red rose's thorn . . . ?"

Charlotte's lip curled in humiliation. "*Dad*, can you please *not*?"

"I know, I know. I am to go away, is it?" Mr. Ramsey said in his goofiest voice. The girls looked at one another and laughed. It was so easy to get embarrassed at whatever your own parents said in front of your friends, even if your friends thought it was hilarious.

"Just ignore me, girls," Mr. Ramsey said. "I'm here for the dog . . . who looks like a Smurf."

"He got blued." Avery giggled.

"All right, I'll get this little rascal cleaned up. You ladies deal with your . . ." Mr. Ramsey winked at Charlotte, ". . . emergency."

"So what's the emergency?" Charlotte asked. Around her, Katani and Isabel had been furiously gathering scraps of paper that Charlotte missed in her quick clean-up and depositing art supplies into their proper containers, while Avery and Maeve—who were utterly useless when it came to matters of cleaning—set up the lemonade, courtesy of Scott Madden.

"Well, I heard it from Maeve," said Katani.

"After Avery called me for some Queen of Romance advice," Maeve added.

"Because Isabel and I soooo can't do this alone anymore," concluded Avery.

Charlotte, confused, shook her head. "Do what? What's going on?"

Isabel took a deep breath and blurted, "Elena Maria dumped Jimmy."

Charlotte threw her arms into the air and screamed, *"Finally!"* Surprised, she covered her mouth. "Was that mean?"

Maeve grinned mischievously. "Maybe . . . but that's *exactly* what I said too!"

"Well, this is great news," Avery chirped. "Now that Elena is single, she and Scott can date, open a restaurant together, fall in love, get married, and we can all eat brownies and live happily ever after!" She attacked the plate of homemade brownies Isabel and Maeve had baked together.

Katani shook her head. "Girl, you are too funny."

Charlotte nodded in agreement. "The writer in me was totally digging that story. Anyway, what's the emergency?"

"It's weird," started Isabel. "Ever since the break up with Jimmy, Elena's been moping around the house." Her voice dropped. "She didn't even want to go to the mall with her best friend, Cammy . . . and they do *everything* together. Scott called last night, and get this—she told me to take a message. She said she was too upset to talk to anyone. I don't know what to do! I mean, she doesn't even like Jimmy anymore. So what's her problem?"

"Well, what does Scott think?" asked Charlotte. As a journalist, she always knew the important questions to ask.

Avery looked grave. "Now that Elena Maria and Jimmy are over but Elena won't talk to Scott on the phone, Scott thinks that she just doesn't like him. I've never seen him so bummed. He's been in the kitchen all day . . . that's what he does when he's depressed . . . cooks."

"How can he not know that she's totally into him?" Katani pondered, chewing thoughtfully on a brownie.

"Sometimes boys just don't get the message, no matter how cute your outfit is," Maeve said wisely.

"Iz? She does like him, right?" Avery probed.

Isabel shrugged and looked at the floor. "I, uh . . . I don't know."

Charlotte tapped her chin with her pencil. "You don't know . . . or you can't *say*?"

Isabel glanced at the ceiling and mumbled, "Um, well . . ."

"Hah!" Avery jumped up and down. "I knew it! She *does* like Scott."

Isabel pretended to zip her lips and throw away the key.

"Okay, okay, be that way. But if we can get those two together in the same room . . . ," Avery began.

"It'll be happily ever after!" Charlotte jumped in.

"But how are we going to get them together? Elena's hardly speaking to anyone," Isabel complained.

"You know," Maeve said, looking around at Charlotte's research materials, "I think I just came up with a brilliant idea."

"Spill, girlfriend!" Katani commanded.

"What about the science fair?" Maeve suggested. "Since you guys are both going to be presenting your projects," she said, looking at Avery and Isabel, "you're going to need a little family support, right? Like from your beloved siblings?"

Avery and Isabel looked at each other. "Perfect!" they shouted, high fiving.

"I am a matchmaking genius," Maeve gushed. "And speaking of matchmaking at the science fair," she went on, "What's all this?" She waved her hand around Charlotte's gallery of posters, then sniffed the air dramatically. "And why do I smell traces of Nick Montoya in here?"

"You do *not*!" Charlotte whacked Maeve lightly with a pillow.

Maeve giggled. "All right, all right, you got me. I saw his name on the corner of your poster. I saw Chelsea's name too, but it's way more fun to tease you about Nick."

"Well," Charlotte answered primly, "you know that I am doing my project with Chelsea and Nick. But we agreed to keep the project a secret until the science fair. If something doesn't work, there's a lot of pressure when three people's grades are riding on it."

"Can you give me a clue?" begged Maeve.

Charlotte shook her head. "My lips are sealed."

"Argh, this is sooo stressing me out!" Avery griped. "I still have all this research to do and you're practically done. Hey, Char, mind if I ask you a few questions?"

Charlotte nodded. She loved being the knowledgeable one. "Go for it."

Maeve prodded Katani and Isabel with a concerned glance. "Hey, while you guys do that, we're going to go have a dinner consultation with your dad. Last sleepover he thought that pizza with mushrooms and clams would be interesting."

"That was a huge mistake!" Katani agreed. She headed out the door, followed closely by Maeve and Isabel.

Avery scurried to the corner to grab a pad of paper and began. "So, Char, what do you know about carbon emissions and stuff?"

Charlotte thought for a minute. "You know what, Avery? You should probably just go online to find this stuff out. That's what Nick and Chelsea and I did when we were researching—oops!" Charlotte clapped both her hands over her mouth. "I almost told you what we're doing! Avery, are all these questions some kind of undercover plot to figure out our secret project? Because it's *not* going to work."

Avery giggled. "*No*, it's not a secret plot. Cross my heart. I actually just really need some help with the research," she admitted.

"Okay," Charlotte answered thoughtfully. "Here's what I did. First, I wrote down a brainstorm list of all the different questions I had. Then, I went online and checked out some books from the library and tried to figure out the answers. *Then*, I called in the expert—Miss Pierce, in my case. But she didn't just tell me the answers right off—she gave me lots of inspiration and helped me figure out stuff for myself, which is way better because I feel like I really understand it now, you know?"

Avery nodded. "So I guess I need to do my own research on carbon emissions . . . even if it's totally not as fun as making loads of gum!" Avery sighed.

Charlotte nodded. "Yup. But if it helps . . . you can totally borrow this book. And here's one of the websites I used . . . I don't think this will give away *too* much about my project," she said, scribbling a Web address on a scrap of paper. "Promise you'll do the research to get all the facts from now on."

Avery spat on her hand and offered it to Charlotte. "Deal."

Charlotte looked horrified and answered, "No way I'm shaking that thing. Come on. Let's go get some dinner."

Substitute Sisters

After one large cheese and one large pepperoni pizza had been fully devoured by the BSG, Mr. Ramsey, and a newly washed Marty-man, the girls laid out their sleeping bags around a crackling fire in the Ramseys' living room.

"Do you remember our very first sleepover? It was right in this exact spot!" Avery reminisced.

"And we all hated each other!" Katani added.

"I still can't believe that," Isabel remarked. She had come to Abigail Adams Junior High a few weeks after school started. By that time Charlotte, Avery, Maeve, and Katani had already started the BSG—and totally got along just fine.

"We have definitely done a lot of growing up since then," noted Charlotte.

"Yes!" Maeve exclaimed, shooting upright in her sleeping bag. "Especially lately."

"What do you mean?" asked Katani.

Maeve blushed. "I don't know. I feel like I understand this whole boy-girl-romance thing more . . ."

Isabel grinned. "But weren't you already 'the expert' on that?"

"Well, now I'm a super-expert!" Maeve laughed. "I've come to understand that crushes can get a little over-the-top. And in other ways too . . ." She eyed her friends and jutted her chin out conspiratorially. "If you know what I mean."

Confused, the BSG looked at each other. "Not really," Avery replied bluntly.

"Like . . ." Maeve's voice dropped to a hush. "Wearing certain things that you didn't, ahem, need to wear before. . . ."

Katani shook her head, and as she did her beaded braids clattered. "You lost me, and I'm supposed to be the expert on who-wears-what around here."

"You know . . . *bras*!" Maeve finally blurted. The girls stared back at her blank-faced, making Maeve wish the floor would open up and swallow her.

"Yeah? What about them?" Avery asked.

Maeve swallowed and took a deep breath. "I, uh . . . okay, big confession here . . . I sort of got one this week. My first one." She looked around at her friends' faces again. She half-expected them to crack up at her but instead they just looked interested.

"Ooo, what's it look like?" Katani asked excitedly. "Did you get one with ribbons? I love those!"

"Well, actually I got two," Maeve explained, slowly getting more excited as she spoke. "One is like a beigy color—and the other one is pink! But really light pink. They have a tiny bit of lace on the straps, and a little bow in front."

"Girl, your taste there was so right. Ribbon decoration is *so* this season," Katani assured her, nodding seriously. Thinking about the bras from Kgirl's straightforward fashion perspective made Maeve feel a whole lot more comfortable. Fashion talk she could handle.

"And the lace on the straps is a slightly lighter color than the rest of it, which looks just lovely, and the bows are actually removable, so if you want you can take them off, like if you're going to wear it under something where the ribbon would show through—"

"Ugh, enough with the lace and bows and stuff!" Avery jumped in. "Here's my personal bra philosophy. Basically, it's the same as my whole philosophy on clothes," she explained with a shrug. "They have to be comfortable. And, oh yeah, be *blue*," she shouted for emphasis. Everyone laughed. "Seriously, it's no big deal. I wear a sports bra—it's just way more comfortable when I'm running up and down the field," explained Avery nonchalantly.

Charlotte jumped in. "What was the shopping like, Maeve?" she asked. "Did you go with your mom? I've been dreading the day when I have to ask my dad to take me bra shopping. That's one of the bad things about not having a mother, I guess." Charlotte's mother had died when she was a little girl. Though Charlotte missed her mother, she understood that it was just a part of life . . . that everyone's family turns out differently. But not having a mother to help her through the girly parts of being a teenager was something she'd always miss.

Maeve gave her friend a sympathetic smile. "You guys know my mom. It turned into this funny scene at the department store. Actually, I don't think I would have made it out of there alive if it hadn't been for Elena Maria." She glanced over at Isabel.

"My sister?" Isabel said, confused. "What did she do?"

"She just happened to be shopping there with Cammy, and she totally saved the day. She showed me where they hide the really adorable, 'age appropriate' bras. FYI, it's in the back, next to the socks."

"She was probably happy to help you, since she hasn't been able to pass on any words of wisdom to *me* yet on that subject," Isabel said. *I'm light years away from that experience,* figured a glum Isabel as she crossed her arms.

"Um, Isabel, everyone gets one sometime," Katani reminded her.

"Right!" Avery agreed.

Maeve turned to Isabel and Katani. "You guys are so lucky you have big sisters to help you out with this stuff. Don't get me wrong, my mom was great, but her style's, well, kind of boring. Moms are aaaaall about being practical, when sometimes you just want to be fun!"

"See, having a sister would solve everything," Charlotte agreed. "Hey guys, I have an idea. Since some of us don't have any sisters to help us out, maybe we can all be each other's substitute sisters when it comes to this whole bra thing."

"I think that's an excellent BSG project!" Katani chimed. "Whenever you wanna go bra shopping, Iz—or anybody—I am happy to volunteer my services."

Avery giggled. "I see what's up. Now that Maeve's officially Queen of Romance and I'm Queen of Gum, Kgirl wants to be Queen of Underwear."

"Har har . . ." Katani rolled her eyes.

"Thanks for the offer, Kgirl," Isabel said with a smile.

Maeve felt a warm glow inside, and it wasn't just because she had her back to the fireplace. She knew she was so lucky to have the BSG. Who else could she talk to about such personal stuff and not feel completely embarrassed?

"You guys are the best substitute sisters ever!" she squealed, giving her fluffy pink pillow a tight squeeze of pure delight.

CHAPTER

18

Red Hair, Green Thumb

First things first. Who's hungry?" Bailey plopped a huge bag on a table in the MIT greenhouse. "I, for one, cannot work on an empty stomach. Plus, I took the liberty of raiding the deli and dessert sections at the dining hall."

Matt's face lit up as he dug into the basket. "What do I owe you?"

"Don't worry about it," Bailey said, with a wave of her hand. "You got the pizza the other day, so this one's on me. Now how about you, Maeve? I have some blueberry muffins. On the other hand, I also have a turkey sub on a French baguette."

"Ooo, turkey for me, please." Maeve wrapped her mouth around the enormous sandwich and took a giant bite. *Forget Matt. Bailey can win me over with deli any day!*

"So Matt says your project is coming along well. Let's see your daffodils . . . ," Bailey said. Maeve and Matt had carried three trays of plants all the way from her kitchen window at her mom's apartment to the MIT greenhouse. Maeve was totally proud of her healthy-looking sprouts. She couldn't wait to see what Bailey had to say about them.

As Bailey inspected the plants carefully, leaning down so that her nose almost brushed the leaves in order to check them out from roots to buds, Maeve held her breath and clasped her hands tightly to keep from biting her nails. She had heaped so much love and care on her plants over the past week. She even kept an exact record of how many times she watered and fertilized each plant. Bailey just had to say they were doing okay!

After what seemed like *hours* to Maeve, Bailey finally stood up. "Maeve, these look very promising, but I think they are going to need a little more light and warmth. You can keep them in the corner of the greenhouse till the science fair, if you want. That way you'll have something very impressive to show your teachers and classmates."

"But how will I take care of them?" Maeve objected, lovingly patting the moist soil around the base of the smallest plant, almost as if she were tucking it into a snuggly, dirt bed. "Don't my sprouts need my attention? I mean, how will I record their progress? My little darlings need me!" She flung herself over the tray, being extra-careful not to bend even one of the growing stalks. After a couple seconds of silence, she opened one eye and peeked at Matt from under her arm.

He and Bailey were smiling. "Think of it this way, Maeve. It's for their own good," he advised her. Maeve stood upright and folded her arms, considering her options.

"Well, if it's what I must do, then it's what I must do," she said with her head held high, feeling just like a classic film heroine. Even more noble than that, actually — Audrey

Hepburn never had to make a decision like this!

Still, Maeve didn't feel totally comfortable leaving her plants here in the greenhouse. On the way over on the T, the trays had bounced up and down in her lap. It took all of her concentration to make sure nothing and no one knocked them off her lap, and for once she didn't even care about getting dirt on her jeans! If her plants were living at MIT, would she still be able to give them the same kind of attention? "They're still kind of small," Maeve explained to Bailey, taking some of the plastic containers off her tray and placing them gently underneath a special greenhouse grow lamp.

"These really are great, Maeve!" Bailey complimented her again. "Are those the control?"

"Yessss," Maeve replied uneasily, glancing at Matt, who gave her an affirming nod. "Control" meant the ones she hadn't given organic fertilizer. Those plants were much smaller.

This news seemed to delight Bailey. "I knew it! I knew it!" she squealed, clapping her hands and dancing around.

Matt laughed. "I haven't seen you this happy since that time you figured out how to program an in-ground water system for your greenhouse!" he joked.

"Hey!" Bailey said. "Who loved that crop of tomatoes more than you?"

Maeve covered her mouth. Matt and this Bailey girl were actually funny when it came to science. She didn't know that such a thing was even possible. And Matt obviously thought Bailey was practically his dream girl . . . even though Maeve still couldn't imagine putting one toe outside her bedroom in some of the stuff Bailey wore. It was clear—Matt was meant for Bailey, not Maeve. Now if only Maeve could find a dude who thought movies *and* raising amazing flowers were cool. Maeve had a growing feeling in the pit of her stomach that between her and Bailey, those daffodils were going to rock and roll.

I guess science to Matt and Bailey is like what movies and plays and getting all dressed up are to me—exciting and fun, Maeve thought. *Although people romance is way more exciting than plant romance. Maybe someone could write a movie about both. There could be this girl who grows the most amazing flowers with her own special organic fertilizer and some handsome guy who owns a big fertilizer company wants to buy her formula . . . and they fall in love and save the world, too. "Love and Blooms."* She could see her name just below the title . . . or maybe above.

"I think you're in excellent shape for the big fair, Maeve," Bailey decided. "A few days under these grow lamps and you'll really see the effects of the special fertilizer."

"Thanks," said Maeve. With the morning sun streaming into the greenhouse, Maeve saw Bailey in a whole new light. In here, her strange, hippy outfit, funny hairdo, and serious knowledge about growing things made her seem like some kind of wise Earth caretaker among her beautiful greenhouse plants. Getting to know her might actually be kind of fun—after all, Maeve loved meeting new people.

Bailey poured a test tube full of tangerine-colored liquid over one of her large flowering plants that was hanging from a ceiling beam. "This is a new nutrient I've been watching compost for months—lemon juice, orange peels, carrots, and of course my secret ingredient."

Matt smiled slyly and teased, "Hey Bail—are you still

trying to get out of eating your fruits and veggies?"

"Hey, I have an idea," Maeve offered. "Do you two want to come to our environmental science fair?" She almost couldn't believe the words were coming out of her mouth.

"You want to?" Bailey asked Matt, her face lighting up.

"Definitely!" Matt exclaimed. "Thanks for the invite, Mix-Master-Curl."

"Oh, you're welcome," Maeve sang sweetly. If this wasn't growing up, then she didn't know what was!

"Let's get your plants all settled in over here. Your dad said he'd pick you up outside," Matt urged. Maeve could have wandered around the greenhouse forever, but it was lunch at Dad's and she didn't want to keep him and Sam waiting. With Bailey and Matt's help, she was ready in a jiff and out the door. She had to hand it to Matt—he picked a great girlfriend.

Listening In

"What in the world are you doing, Charlotte?" asked Mr. Ramsey. Charlotte was lying flat on the Oriental rug in their den with her ear pressed to the floor.

"I'm trying to see if Miss Pierce is still awake. I want to run down and talk to her about my project."

Mr. Ramsey chuckled. "Do you really think that's such a hot idea, Char? It's nine o'clock."

"But Dad, I want to update her on how my project is coming and return this—ah hah! I just heard footsteps. She must still be up." Charlotte shot up from her post and ran into the kitchen. Thirty seconds later she returned carrying a tray with a teapot full of hot cocoa and a plate of sugar cookies.

Mr. Ramsey looked at his daughter in awe. "I know I don't say this a lot, but this is exactly something your mother would've done. She was always very thoughtful to friends and neighbors . . . particularly older people."

Charlotte smiled. "Thanks, Dad."

"Charlotte, what are you doing still awake?" Miss Pierce asked when she opened the door. Charlotte heard beautiful music from inside the apartment, like a Spanish guitar. Miss Pierce was wearing a long, white nightgown and holding a book called *The Chemistry of Cakes*.

"Is this a bad time? I didn't wake you, did I?"

"No, not at all. I was having a little trouble sleeping, actually, so I decided to catch up on my reading. I'm learning all about the science of food. Fascinating."

Charlotte beamed. "Well, I have just the thing for trouble sleeping. Hot cocoa made with milk. My dad used to give this to me to help me fall asleep when we traveled." Charlotte loved all the adventures she and her dad had had, living all over the world, but she was very happy now that she had a place to call home.

Charlotte poured herself and Miss Pierce two dainty little cups of cocoa and took a seat on the couch.

"So, Charlotte, to what do I owe this pleasant surprise?"

"Well," Charlotte began, "I just wanted to tell you that I'm making really good progress on my part of the project. In fact, I'm almost finished!"

"Why, Charlotte, that's wonderful!" Miss Pierce exclaimed. "I'm so proud of your work on this project. Sometimes you remind me of myself as a girl, do you know that?"

Charlotte felt herself glowing with pride. "If I decide to

become a scientist, I hope I can be as good at it as you are, Miss Pierce," she said softly.

"I am quite certain that you will be even better!" Miss Pierce assured her with a smile. "As long as you are never afraid to ask questions . . . and never afraid to go out and find the answers."

Charlotte nodded, then remembered one of the reasons she had come down in the first place. "Oh!" Charlotte pulled something out of her purse. "Here's the book you loaned me. It really helped. Avery took a look at it too. You saved our lives!"

"Oh, Charlotte!" Miss Pierce exclaimed. "I'd hardly call what I did *life saving*. Besides, you did all that work yourself. I just lent you a book."

"Well, it was very helpful, then," Charlotte insisted. "Really. Nick and Chelsea and I never would have come up with the great idea for our project if it hadn't been for you!"

"Chelsea . . ." Miss Pierce scratched her forehead. "Now she's the lovely girl who takes all the pictures for your paper?"

"That's right!" How easily Charlotte could forget that although Miss Pierce kept to herself a lot, she still knew just about everything going on in the Beacon Street neighborhood.

"And Nick . . . is that young Nicholas Montoya?"

Charlotte felt her cheeks burning. "Yes."

Miss Piece smiled. "I remember that boy when he was just a little tyke. Back when I used to frequent Montoya's Bakery. What a handsome young man he is now, though. Wouldn't you agree?"

Charlotte shrugged and into her tea cup mumbled, "I don't know . . . I guess . . . maybe so."

Miss Pierce raised an eyebrow and gave Charlotte a wink. "Maybe so, indeed."

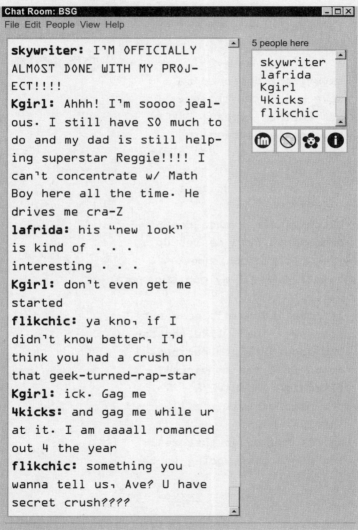

4kicks: not ME, sicko! EW.
No. Scott is still moping
around this house like Eeyore
lafrida: same w/Elena. She
keeps saying she'd rather be
a chef than date.
skywriter: oh for pete's
sake . . . can those 2 just
get 2gether already!!!!???
4kicks: no kidding
Kgirl: I thought you girls
were going to get them
together @ the science
fair???
4kicks: yeah I made scott
promise to help me set up
. . . it's a punishment . . .
he ate like, ½ my gum supplies
lafrida: EM hasn't gone out
all week. she's like obsess-
ing about all her recipes. I
dunno if I can convince!!
flikchic: you HAVE 2!! In
the name of LOVE, Iz!!!
lafrida: how?
Kgirl: how about just telling her Scott's going to be
there??

5 people here

skywriter
lafrida
Kgirl
4kicks
flikchic

skywriter: the truth! I love it. So insane it just might work

lafrida: No that would never work . . . she's in the "I'm avoiding all boys right now" stage

4kicks: Blindfold her and put her in a wheelbarrow. Say it's a surprise

Kgirl: That's called kidnap-ping, Avery!

flikchic: what if you just say you want her there for sisterly support?

lafrida: not bad . . .

4kicks: and if that doesn't work . . . plan B is wheel-barrow

skywriter: NO!

lafrida: NO!

Kgirl: NO!

flikchic: NO!

4kicks: KIDDING!

5 people here

skywriter
lafrida
Kgirl
4kicks
flikchic

CHAPTER

19

Blue Sludge

𝒜very felt like a gum zombie as she lugged her enormous backpack and a giant, foldable foam core poster down Beacon Street to Abigail Adams Junior High. Her feet might as well have had lead blocks tied to them at the rate she was going.

"Hey, Avery! Wait up!" sang a voice behind her. It was Maeve, jogging as fast as she could, which was a pretty hilarious scene. Her wild red hair was blowing everywhere in the sharp, spring wind, and the long, pink scarf she was wearing (a gift from Katani) kept blowing up into her face. "Blegh! I got cotton in my mouth!" she groaned, batting at the fabric. "So what's with all the stuff?"

"Science project," Avery managed. "Stayed up all night to finish. Tired. Very tired."

Maeve nodded. For once she'd finished all her work on the assignment early. She'd turned in her lab reports and had set up her station the day before. Partly it was due to Bailey and Matt's enthusiastic encouragement. But Maeve had actually done all the grunt work herself. She had actually really enjoyed taking care of her plants. Maybe if she didn't make it in Hollywood, she could have a back-up career as a horticulturalist actress. *So many options.* Maeve was comforted by that thought.

It felt amazing to be home free before anyone else. She wanted to brag a little, but her mom always told her nobody likes a bragger. Plus, this might just be a once-in-a-lifetime occurrence. After the science fair project was done, Maeve might be right back doing the procrastination thing, just like Avery. She didn't want to jinx herself.

It wasn't often that Maeve could outrun, let alone outwalk Avery. She glanced back to see if maybe someone had attached heavy chains to her speediest friend's feet. She was a little surprised by what she saw instead. "Ave, so this shoe business . . . are you trying to make a statement, or are you just losing your mind?"

"Huh?" Avery glanced down. "Oh, you have got to be *kidding me!*" On one foot she was wearing one of her favorite bright orange running shoes, and on the other she had a bright blue high-top. "I look like a crazy person."

Maeve smiled and threw her arm around Avery's shoulder. "Well, you're my favorite crazy person. C'mon, let's go." And the girls skipped the rest of the way, perfectly in sync.

They arrived at school and made a beeline straight for the gym, where their classmates were hard at work setting up their projects. Maeve was thrilled to be done—it gave her a chance to mosey around the room and check out the cool things that other kids had come up with. Some projects were really awesome, but others, she thought, were kind of lame—like Pete

Wexler's cloud diorama, which was supposed to show how jet fuel can pollute clouds but was really just some cotton balls in a shoe box. Anna and Joline had teamed up to do a project about which brand of eyeliner lasted the longest. Their poster looked a little like Maeve's face after she cried so much about Matt. "Uh, just wondering, but what does this have to do with the environment?" Maeve asked them.

"We only used eyeliners that weren't tested on animals," Anna haughtily explained.

"Duh," added Joline.

Maeve had to muster up all of her strength not to burst out laughing. Joline was wearing green eyeliner with big gobs of tacky glitter, and Anna was sporting bright neon blue. The girls looked like they'd escaped from a clown colony. Now she knew what her mom meant by *too much makeup*. And what did products not tested on animals really have to do with the environment? But actually, looking more closely at Anna and Joline's poster, Maeve had to admit their research was pretty good. They *had* tested just about every eyeliner on the market.

The Trentini twins had made an exploding minivolcano. Maeve thought it was really cool to see it explode over and over again, and interesting to read about how volcanoes put gases into the atmosphere that could have effects in a totally different part of the world. The twins' poster informed her that in 1815, a volcanic eruption in Indonesia caused frosts during July in Europe, halfway around the world! "Did you see this?" Maeve asked Charlotte, pulling her friend over to the twins' booth.

Charlotte, however, had seen a ton of science fairs. She

said with a laugh, "You know, I've gone to school in Paris and Australia and no matter where on earth I turn up . . . *someone* always makes a volcano for the science fair."

Isabel's artistic study of phytoplankton was absolutely breathtaking. She'd done an informative and thorough study of how global warming affected the algae, and the important role the algae played in the health of the oceans. It seemed that all her viewers were so captivated by her radiant illustrations they were actually getting really interested in her research, too.

"Well, if I learned anything today, it's that art can really inspire people to care about something. That's so cool!" Isabel gushed.

"Totally," Avery agreed. "If I had any artistic talent, I would definitely use it to get everyone fired up about all kinds of important causes."

"That's why we all have to stick together," Maeve proclaimed. "So we can all use our different talents to help each other do whatever we want to do."

"I like that!" Charlotte agreed.

"Example: as the ultimate gum chef slash wizard, I can provide you all with a lifetime supply of Avery Madden's Green Tea Lime Fusion gum!" Avery cried. Everyone laughed. "C'mon. Come with me." Avery led Charlotte, Maeve, and Isabel to the massive stand she had prepared in the corner. It looked like a gum shrine—she had tried to document every kind of gum that she had created by sticking goopy wads all over the poster.

"It looks a little . . . ," Isabel started, not sure how to say what she was thinking.

"Gross?" Avery suggested. Isabel nodded. "Yeah, I wanted my poster to be all natural—no glue, you know? So I just had Scott chew all the gum till it was soft and then I stuck it to the foam core. But it didn't turn out quite as scientific-looking as I pictured it in my head."

The girls giggled. "That must be the Tru Blu, right?" Charlotte asked, pointing to a huge wad of electric blue gum stuck in the middle of all of Avery's earth-toned samples.

"I call it Blue Sludge!" Avery announced. "Can you imagine actually putting that garbage in your body?"

Charlotte trembled. "Scaaary. Only Avery's natural gum for me from now on!" she declared.

"And me," added a voice behind them.

The girls turned to see Katani grab one of Avery's free samples from the bowl she had put out on a table. "I got to admit," started Avery, "even though we aren't fighting about the gum factory anymore, I still didn't exactly expect you to support my cause."

Katani shrugged. "I checked out the links you sent me to those rain forest and nutrition sites. You're right—all the preservatives and artificial stuff in that Tru Blu gum are gross."

"Whoa, wait a sec, Kgirl. Did you just say I'm *right?*" Avery asked.

Katani looked serious. "Well, we're both right. Cutting down on packaging would be better for the enviro, and using chicle in gum is better for my bod *and* the rain forest economy—but I still think the gum factory will be good for the economy here in Boston."

"And, um, actually . . . you're right about another thing," Avery admitted. "I *should* have done better research. When

Mr. Moore asked me to look into the factory's carbon emissions, I found out that they already have a really solid plan for reducing their carbon footprint. The factory's going to be really energy efficient."

"So . . . ?" Katani prompted her. "You're not trying to shut down the factory anymore?"

"Nope. But I am trying to get them to relocate so they're closer to the T and change how they package their gum. Mr. Moore really likes my report, and he said he's going to get in touch with some people he knows on the city council. Maybe the Green Machine can really make a difference!"

"That's so great, Avery!" Charlotte congratulated her.

"Thanks! So if the factory ends up making those changes, then I guess I can live with Tru Blu, as long as they keep their carbon emissions low. But Avery Madden's natural Green Tea Lime Fusion is still the only thing *I'm* chewing."

"I'll agree with that!" Katani said with a grin, high-fiving Avery.

Suddenly a familiar voice echoed over the loudspeaker in the gym. "Attention, students," Mrs. Field's calm but firm voice commanded them. "May I have just a moment of your time for an announcement from one of our janitors, Mr. Clauson." There was a pause, and the BSG exchanged looks. What was this about?

"This announcement is in regard to the 'gum wars' some of you have been waging in the halls of our fine school," Mr. Clauson intoned after a pause. Avery gulped. "I am asking you to stop this silliness immediately. No more gum on the stairs. No more gum on the floor. And especially no more gum on the chairs! I don't care if it's green or blue or purple paisley polka-dotted—if I see one more sticky, icky, chewed-up and spit-out piece, there *will* be consequences." The loudspeaker clicked off.

"I hope that's the end of that!" Katani declared.

"It is from my end, you got my word," Avery agreed. "This gum war is officially over!"

"So what did you end up doing your project on, Katani?" Charlotte asked.

"Check it out!" Katani motioned for the girls to follow her over to the table she had set up on the other side of the gym. "I call it . . . mood lighting."

The girls all oohed at once. Katani had made several little dioramas that looked like tiny rooms and had placed different-colored lights in each. They were tiny colorful bulbs—like Christmas tree lights. "You know how Kelley is very sensitive to lights?" Katani asked.

"Yeah. I once saw this thing on the Discovery Channel that said that people with autism have superpower senses," Isabel recalled.

"Well, we end up using up a lot of power in my house because of Kelley's special light requests. The lights in my project run completely on energy generated by water power. See?" Katani opened a water valve and a little fountain of water began running and turned on a pink light in a little model bedroom.

"That is so cool, Katani!" Charlotte gasped.

"You know," Maeve agreed, "pink lighting makes people feel better."

The girls laughed. "I mean, it's cool that you did a project that is not only good for the environment, but good for all families with someone who has autism," Charlotte said with a smile.

"I also calculated the amount of money and energy you can save by changing all the light bulbs in your house to CFBs—compact florescent bulbs," Katani went on. "They're pretty incredible. They use seventy-five percent less energy and last for up to ten times as long! Changing light bulbs is something every family can do."

"That really is truly fabulous, Kgirl," Maeve complimented her. Isabel and Charlotte just shook their heads in amazement. Katani always put everything she had into projects; this might be her best one yet.

Isabel jokingly poked Charlotte. "So when do we get to see this incredible secret project that you, Nick, and Chelsea are doing?"

Charlotte zipped her lips mysteriously. "We are setting up in a top secret location."

"Top secret, eh?" Avery craftily rubbed her hands together. "Bet it won't be so top secret when I find it myself. Come on, girls!" she teased, egging on the rest of the BSG to follow her on a mission. Maeve and Isabel giggled and skipped after Avery.

A look of panic struck Charlotte's face. "Wait! Stop!" she cried, half laughing, as she ran out behind them.

Katani didn't have time for an undercover science detective mission right now. She still had a lot of work to do on her display to make it just perfect. Out of the corner of her eye she noticed Reggie, a few booths down, putting the final touches on his very dramatic project—a model go-cart track that used only hybrid carts, powered both by fuel and batteries. Katani had to admit, she'd felt slightly jealous at the number of kids who had gushed over Reggie's display. It was pretty flashy, complete with rock music and colorful, blinking lights. Katani's project looked modest in comparison, but she had worked very hard and had gotten every detail just right.

She mustered up all of her acting skills—if only she could morph into a different person like Maeve—and pretended to be totally cool and nonchalant as she sauntered over to Reggie's booth. Up close, Reggie's project was even more impressive. The go-cart track was so perfect, Katani thought, it was a shame that there wasn't a population of two-inch tall people to enjoy all his hard work. He had decorated the track with tiny flags and painted everything perfectly—it almost looked like a mini-carnival! Katani stared at the track. *This boy genius is too amazing!* she fumed to herself. Reggie was so busy fiddling around with batteries and wires on the floor that he didn't even notice her subtle inspection.

Just then, she caught sight of Reggie's calculations for how much battery power the cars would require. Katani might not have been very good at acting, but she was exceptional at math. And it didn't take her long to figure out that one of Reggie's calculations was off. She did a little quick math on the pad of paper she was carrying and realized that if Reggie applied his work, those go-carts weren't going to get very far. Suddenly Katani felt bad for the little two-inch people she had imagined, because if they actually existed, they wouldn't have a very fun time at Reggie DeWitt's go-cart track when their carts ran out of battery power!

She felt a surge of smugness and superiority to that know-it-all science geek who had oh-so-rudely borrowed her very own father. *This'll show him that he's not as smart as he thinks!* Katani gloated to herself.

"Cool project, man," Dillon exclaimed as he passed by Reggie's booth.

"Yeah!" Henry Yurt added. "For once I wish I was shorter so I could, like, ride on this stuff!" He gave Reggie an enthusiastic high-five.

Katani folded her arms and prepared for her moment of sweet revenge. She was going to point out Reggie's flaming error in front of two of his fans. He would be so humiliated! She smiled and began, "I was reading your calculations, Reggie—"

"Oh, yeah!" Reggie jumped up from the floor with a huge smile on his face. Katani's heart thumped. He looked so happy . . . and kind of cute. "Um, uh, I was reading your calculations too, actually." Katani tilted her head. Was it just her imagination, or was Reggie actually *nervous*?

"Your work with water power is so fascinating . . . I mean, uh . . . really sick, man," Reggie corrected himself quickly.

Katani frowned. "Sick?" Was he for real? When would Reggie quit with this whole ridiculous rap star persona?

"Yeah, you know. Sick—like awesome. Off the hook! Sick is better than sweet. Your project rocks the house, Katani."

Whoa. The way he said it was total goofball (really, as if Kgirl didn't know what "sick" meant!), but his compliment was actually . . . nice. She felt so rattled all of a sudden that she didn't know quite what to say except a soft, "Thank you."

"I wish your booth was farther away, actually," Reggie went on. "It kind of makes me look bad. You have this like, important idea that could actually help people, and I just have a model toy set."

At that moment Katani didn't want to humiliate Reggie at all. "Yours is sick too, Reggie. You did, uh . . . a great job," she told him, feeling the white lie stick a little in her throat. Now Katani didn't know what to do. Should she tell him about the mistake in his calculations? Maybe it would be better just to let it go. Most people would never even notice the error when they looked at his project . . .

"I hope so," he confided. "Ms. R wants me to do a live demonstration at the Science Fair tomorrow night."

"That's gonna rock, dude!" Dillon said enthusiastically, high-fiving Reggie.

Katani gulped as she realized what was going to happen. When he demonstrated his project in front of the entire school, he was going to be humiliated for sure! Everyone would watch his perfect little go-carts run out of battery power and stop right in the middle of the demonstration. Katani opened her mouth to say something, but when she looked at Dillon and Yurt's excited faces, she closed it again. Warning Reggie now, in front of his admirers, was just as bad. She swallowed, feeling absolutely terrible for Math Boy, and said in a voice she hoped sounded optimistic, "Good luck!" And to herself she added, *he's gonna need it.*

CHAPTER

20

Symbiotic Relationships

"Eeeeleeeenaaaaa," Isabel yelled, "I'm running mega late for the science fair!" She pushed her way into their bedroom and gaped in horror. "And so are you!" She pointed at Elena Maria, who was wrapped up in her fuzzy purple terry cloth bathrobe. "Will you get dressed? You can't go to the science fair in your PJs."

Elena Maria crawled back under her comforter. "I'm not going to the science fair, okay?"

Isabel threw back her head. She and Avery had been plotting this forever—the final step in their matchmaking plot. "Are you kidding me? You're going to ruin everything!"

Elena Maria sat up with a start. "*I'm* going to ruin everything? What are you talking about? This is your science fair, Iz."

"I, um, I know that," stammered Isabel. "I just mean that if you don't go you will ruin the family support vibe. And that vibe is, um, very, *very* important to me. I mean Mom is going to a play this evening, I don't want her to have to cancel her plans."

"Oh, for pete's sake," groaned Elena Maria. "As much as I want to help your . . . whadya call it . . . family vibe, going to anything tonight is seriously the last thing I want to do."

Isabel sat down on the edge of her sister's bed. "How come? Tell your dear sister all about it."

"Don't tease me tonight—I'm not in the mood." Elena Maria blinked and Isabel noticed that her sister's eyes were pink and swollen. "At lunch today Jimmy asked a girl to the spring dance . . . right before my very eyes!"

Isabel puckered her lower lip in sympathy. "Oh, Elena. That's horrible. I'm so sorry."

"It gets worse." Elena Maria sniffled. "The girl he asked out was Cammy Dooley, my supposed best friend!" She blew her nose into a tissue.

"Cammy Dooley!" Isabel squeaked. "You've got to be kidding!"

"Now my *ex*-best friend," Elena Maria huffed. "Well, you know what? She can have dweebish Jimmy, and his dweebish friends, and I hope she has a lot of dweebish fun making dweebish food for the dweebish indoor lacrosse team!" She got out of bed and began furiously brushing her long, silky hair. "I might as well just get used to the fact that I'm going to end up an old maid living with a million cats."

Isabel rolled her eyes. "You hate cats, Elena . . . and you don't even like Jimmy anymore, anyway. You said so."

"That's totally not the point. The point is . . ." Elena Maria looked tragically at her reflection in the mirror. "The point is I am a failure at romance. I'm going to be alone forever. Now if you'll excuse me, I must go downstairs. If you need me I'll be in the kitchen, baking away my pain."

"Okay." Isabel shrugged. "Hey, speaking of baking . . . Avery said Scott baked a huge cake designed to look like a gumball."

Elena Maria froze at her door. "He did?"

Isabel smiled. "Yup. He's bringing it to the fair tonight."

Elena Maria turned her head slowly. "He is?"

"Yup. He mentioned that he hoped you'd be there—he wants another cook's professional opinion."

A smug smile popped on Elena Maria's face. "He does? That's so sweet. Well, I'd hate to let him down. You know, as one professional to another." Elena Maria untied her robe to reveal an adorable khaki pleated skirt and a crisp, white blouse. "Yikes, would you look at the time! Isabel, clap clap, let's *go!*"

Isabel was so stunned by her sister's caterpillar to butterfly transformation that she was utterly speechless. *If time heals all wounds, then my sister should be in* The Guinness Book of World Records! she thought. "Okay, let's go!"

Matchmaker, Matchmaker

"Step right up, ladies and gentle-dudes," Avery cried. "Step right up! See the amazing gum-chewing super boy. The one and only, the great . . . *Scottdini!*"

"Ave—this will require major compensation later, of the chore-doing kind," Scott whispered in his sister's ear as he squeezed her elbow. He was totally mortified by Avery's carnival-style presentation.

"I'll tell you why he rules the kingdom of gum," Avery continued to shout. "Because . . . he's *Scottdini.* Emperor of stickiness. Sultan of spearmint. King of the environment."

Scott stepped off the footstool. "That's it, I'm leaving."

Avery sighed. She'd tried every trick in the book to find Elena Maria. She'd sent Scott over to Isabel's booth to ask for tape, but he said that Isabel wasn't there. Then there was her last idea—making Scott into a circus sideshow in hopes that Elena Maria would see him. Twenty minutes later, the only people who had found Scott were two giggly sixth graders who wanted their pictures taken with "the great Scottdini."

"Aw, c'mon, bro. Don't leave . . . ," Avery begged.

Scott glared at Avery. "How do I put this? Okay, remember when I hurt my leg skiing last winter? And I had to spend the entire ski weekend in a hospital with that crazy nurse who practiced opera singing in my room?"

Avery nodded nervously.

"Tonight is making me miss that nurse." Scott glumly took a seat on the stool. "Are you sure Elena Maria said she wanted my chocolate dipped granola banana recipe? I feel like she's not even coming."

Avery shrugged. "That's what Isabel told me. I mean, uh . . . you know how Elena likes her bananas." *Bananas.* Avery shuddered. *I'm the one who's bananas.* She felt a little guilty about making that last part up, but Avery was tired of seeing her brother mope around the house like a love-sick puppy. Desperate times called for desperate measures, and the desperate one in this situation was Avery!

She cleared her throat and gave one last hearty, "Come and see the great Scottdini!"

"Since when is your brother a magician?" asked Charlotte with a coy smile. She was sort of an amateur magician herself and had become quite good at performing tricks in public.

"They're not called magicians, they're *illusionists*," corrected Isabel, who also seemed to have appeared out of nowhere.

"He's not a magician, he's a gum artist," Avery clarified. "And, *ahem*, where in the name of Scottdini have you been, Isabel?" She lowered her voice and added, "I *thought* you were bringing company."

"I did, but it wasn't easy," Isabel whispered back. "She went into the bathroom fifteen minutes ago to check on her lip gloss and I haven't seen her s—"

"*Yo, Elena Maria! Over here!*" Avery interrupted. She started jumping up and down and waving her hands furiously in the air. Elena Maria, standing at the far end of the gym, looked positively terrified as she crept over to Avery's booth.

"That was slick, Sis," Scott growled. His face was pinker than Maeve's bedroom.

"Hi," Elena Maria greeted them softly, as she reached the booth. She looked around at Avery's display. "So . . . where's the cake?"

Scott, Avery, and Charlotte looked bewildered. "What cake?" Avery asked. "You want some gum or something?"

Elena Maria blinked. "Scott's cake. That's why you wanted me here, right?"

Scott scratched his head. "I thought you came over here for my chocolate dipped bananas recipe."

Elena Maria made a gagging noise. "Ew, no! I hate bananas."

Scott shook his head and started to say, "But Avery told

me . . ." just as Elena Maria was explaining, "But Isabel told me . . ."

"Uh-oh!" Charlotte felt a giggle escape from her mouth. "I mean, uh, you guys . . . want to see my project?"

Avery and Isabel glanced at each other, nodded, and took a giant step back. They didn't walk over to Charlotte's booth—they *ran*, leaving Scott and Elena alone to untangle Avery and Isabel's little white lies.

"You two are officially the world's worst matchmakers," Charlotte declared.

Isabel and Avery looked at each other and burst out laughing. "That's it. I'm retiring from matchmaking forever," Avery vowed.

"Me, too," agreed Isabel. "Although . . ." She tilted her head towards Avery's booth, where Scott and Elena Maria were sitting side by side on the pair of stools and merrily chatting away. "Somehow I think we just might have pulled it off."

"What is it about science fairs that makes people get together?" Charlotte wondered out loud.

"What do you mean?" Isabel asked.

Charlotte pointed to Katani's booth. "Call me crazy, but those two 'sworn enemies' are looking awfully friendly . . ."

The girls looked over and saw Reggie, who had shed his over-sized hoodie to reveal khakis and a sweater vest, standing at Katani's booth. "What happened to those ridiculous baggy pants he's been wearing for the past month?" Charlotte asked.

Isabel giggled and shook her head. "I don't know, but I'm glad they're gone!" Then the girls watched, open-mouthed, as the newly clean-cut Reggie presented Katani with a yellow long-stemmed rose. Avery threw her arms in the air. "I swear I had *nothing* to do with that!"

Katani, standing stiffly behind her booth, was even more shocked than Avery. "What's this supposed to be?" she demanded.

Reggie looked serious. "Um, it's . . . you know . . . a rose." For once he had stopped using that stupid fake voice and just sounded like regular old Reggie DeWitt.

"I know it's a rose . . . ," Katani replied, sounding slightly irritated. "But what does it mean?" Maeve might have been okay with wildly romantic gestures, but they made Katani downright uncomfortable.

Reggie quickly assured her, "Yellow roses are symbolic for friendship. I read it in this horticulture book I have," he added shyly, then went on, "and after what you did today, I figured I could call you a friend."

"What did I do?" Katani asked innocently.

Reggie reached into his pocket and pulled out a piece of lined paper. "I got an anonymous tip today. Apparently my go-cart equations were off. Whoever wrote this *totally* saved my life . . . or at least my reputation. And there's only one person at this school who knows math like I do."

"Who's that?" Katani squeaked.

Reggie looked her straight in the eye. "Well, that's you, Katani." He placed the flower on her table. "And now I feel like a total idiot. I spent all this time wearing these stupid pants that were constantly about to fall down and talking funny and spending time with your dad to impress you, when I should have just been focused on the math. I mean, let's face it, I'm not cool. I'm just Math Boy. Anyway, I hope you don't hate me," he mumbled, and started walking away.

Katani stared at the back of his head for a second, too shocked to speak. He had been wearing all that crazy hip-hop gear and hanging out with her dad . . . to *impress* her? What did that mean? Finally she found her voice and called out, "Hey, Reggie!"

He turned around slowly. "Yeah?"

"Um . . . thanks for the rose." She picked it up and smiled. "Actually, I like Math Boy a lot better than Rap Boy."

Reggie just grinned at her and walked away, leaving Katani's heart beating a mile a minute. She tried to focus on the lovely friendship rose, and not that other pesky, annoying thought . . . the one about what a more-than-friendship rose might be like.

Katani, feeling very unlike her normal self, wandered over to the one person who could possibly bring her back to earth.

"I saw that!" Maeve squealed as Katani approached. "I know what you're going to say—yellow rose means friend-ship and blah blah blah, but come *on*, Katani! It's soooo obvi-ous that Reggie DeWitt is totally into you."

"I've landed." Katani sighed. "Maeve, you know, there is such a thing as a guy and a girl being just friends. Besides, Reggie DeWitt is totally not my type. He's way too into school-work, he thinks he's the smartest person in the world, and he always has to be the best."

Maeve smirked. "Hmmm, who does that sound like? . . . You!"

Katani opened her mouth to protest and then began to

laugh. "Okay, okay, fine. But how about this? If Reggie and I are the same, then there's no way he could like me. Isn't it true that opposites attract?"

"I used to think that . . . ," Maeve glanced dreamily at Matt and Bailey, who were checking out the displays like kids in a candy store. It was hard to tell who was more excited about the AAJH Science Fair. "But now I think that a lot of times, people get together because they like to do the same things."

Matt and Bailey waltzed over to Maeve's booth with their arms intertwined. "Wow, Maeve! Thanks for inviting us. These experiments are wonderful. Of course, I think yours takes the cake," Bailey said with a wink.

"I couldn't agree more," said a voice behind her. Maeve turned around to see Mr. Moore. She was completely surprised. Did she just get a compliment on her work from a teacher . . . a *science* teacher? "Your display is well-presented, Maeve, and your research appears very solid. I'm pleased that you added to your excellent research by reaching out to an expert." He nodded at Bailey. "I can tell you put a lot of effort into this, Maeve."

"She did, sir," Matt jumped in. He gave Maeve a little secret thumbs-up as Mr. Moore looked over at the plants again. Maeve felt a grin cover her face from ear to ear. She had never felt so proud of a school project in her whole life.

"Keep up the good work," Mr. Moore told her, smiling and moving onto the next booth.

"Congrats, Mix-Master-Curl!" Matt cried, giving Maeve a high five. "Sounds like you just got an A."

Bailey put an arm around Matt's waist. "You deserve it, Maeve," she agreed.

Seeing Matt and Bailey so happy together put Maeve's whole dream-crush situation in perspective. Maeve knew that someday she'd meet a guy who'd turn her perfect dream-crush into reality. And you just couldn't rush that kind of perfect.

"Bad news, bubba," said Bailey, tugging on Matt's sleeve. "We gotta run or we'll be late for the movie. My club, Students for Environmental Action, is showing an awesome documentary on global warming," she explained.

"But I don't want to leave," Matt whined jokingly.

"Me neither, but as president of SEA I have to be present at all club events." Bailey and Matt waved good-bye to Katani and Maeve and *slowly* made their way out the door.

Maeve looked smugly at Katani. "Still think opposites attract?"

Katani knew she'd been beaten and smiled. "Maybe not."

Maeve grabbed Katani's hand. "But just in case you still have any doubt . . . follow me." She dragged Katani to a huge crowd that had gathered in one corner of the gym. Chelsea, Charlotte, and Nick Montoya were giving a live demonstration of their project—a green campsite. They had managed to borrow equipment from all sorts of hiking stores. They had solar-powered grills and showers, tents made of 100 percent recycled products, organic food, and bug repellent. Charlotte had made a diagram demonstrating how portable solar panels could be used to power an entire campsite.

People were so pumped by their demonstration that they were signing up for a solar camping trip to be led by Charlotte, Nick, Chelsea, Mr. Ramsey, Mr. Moore, Ms. R . . . and the Crow! Katani noticed that even though all three kids were having a great time leading the group, Charlotte and Nick had a special connection—they always had—due to their mutual love of travel and exploration. Katani made a note to tell Maeve that common interests might be the basis of true romance.

"Attention," called Mrs. Fields as Mr. Moore wheeled a huge monitor onto the stage. "Attention, everyone. We have a very special surprise for you all." She turned on the TV and a face familiar to the BSG appeared on the screen. It was Sally Ride, the world famous astronaut, congratulating the school for taking the time to learn about the environment and proving that science can be fun.

Katani and Maeve squeezed their way over to Isabel and Avery. "How is Reggie DeWitt?" Avery whispered to Katani in a sing-songy voice.

Maeve put her finger over Avery's lips and pointed to the screen. "This is supposed to about science, Avery. Have some respect!"

Katani gave her a grateful look, and Maeve knew that her mother was right . . . she *was* growing up.

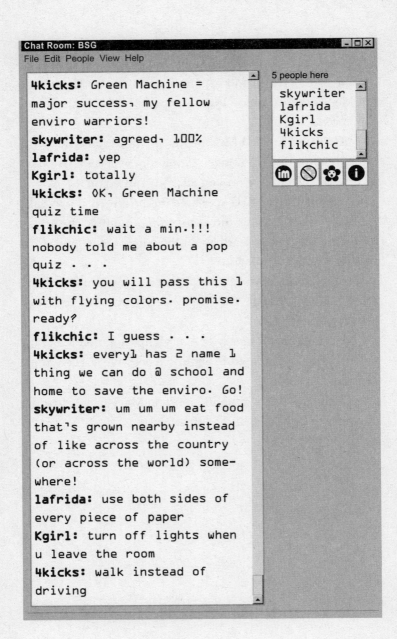

Chat Room: BSG

File Edit People View Help

4kicks: Green Machine = major success, my fellow enviro warriors!

skywriter: agreed, 100%

lafrida: yep

Kgirl: totally

4kicks: OK, Green Machine quiz time

flikchic: wait a min.!!! nobody told me about a pop quiz . . .

4kicks: you will pass this 1 with flying colors. promise. ready?

flikchic: I guess . . .

4kicks: every1 has 2 name 1 thing we can do @ school and home to save the enviro. Go!

skywriter: um um um eat food that's grown nearby instead of like across the country (or across the world) somewhere!

lafrida: use both sides of every piece of paper

Kgirl: turn off lights when u leave the room

4kicks: walk instead of driving

5 people here

skywriter
lafrida
Kgirl
4kicks
flikchic

Green Algae and Bubble Gum Wars

BOOK EXTRAS

Trivialicious Trivia

Book Club Buzz

Charlotte's Word Nerd Dictionary

green algae and bubble gum wars
trivialicious trivia

1. What is Matt's nickname for Maeve?
   A. Maevester
   B. Maevey-Baby
   C. Mix-Master-Curl
   D. Little Red

2. Who offers to watch Sam at the Sally Ride Science Festival?
   A. Matt
   B. Bailey
   C. Charlotte
   D. Maeve

3. Who is Sally Ride?
   A. The new AAJH science teacher
   B. An MIT professor
   C. Matt's girlfriend
   D. The first American female astronaut to go into space

4. Bailey uses her special fertilizer to grow what kind of plant?
   A. Sunflowers
   B. Peonies
   C. Green beans
   D. Roses

5. Which celebrity is endorsing Tru Blu Gum?
   A. Audrey Hepburn
   B. Madonna
   C. Jake Axle
   D. Caleb Tucker

6. Who does Charlotte ask for help with her science project?
   A. Mrs. Fields
   B. Mr. Ramsey
   C. Matt
   D. Miss Pierce

7. What is the name of the group that makes snacks for Jimmy's lacrosse team?
   A. The Snackers
   B. The Snack Club
   C. Snack Attack
   D. The Food Group

8. What can't Avery's gum do?
   A. Stick to things
   B. Taste good
   C. Contain sugar
   D. Create bubbles

9. What is wrong with Reggie's science project?
   A. One of the calculations is wrong
   B. It has nothing to do with the environment
   C. He left it at home
   D. Nothing

10. What color is the rose that Reggie gives Katani?
    A. red
    B. white
    C. yellow
    D. pink

Book Club Buzz

10 QUESTIONS FOR YOU AND YOUR FRIENDS TO CHAT ABOUT

1. Have you ever done a science fair project? If so, what did you do? What's the most fun science project you can think of?

2. Reggie's new wardrobe and attitude annoy Katani. Why do you think Reggie changed the way he dressed and acted? Have you ever changed the way you dressed or acted in order to seem cooler or fit in?

3. Maeve is unsure about wearing a bra, and at first she feels like she doesn't have anyone to talk to about it. Who can you talk to about growing up? What are some questions that you have?

4. Isabel and Avery play matchmaker by getting Elena Maria and Scott together. Do you think

it was a good idea for them to do that? What
do you think could have happened if their
plan backfired?

5. Kiki Underwood's dad gets a pop star to en-
dorse Tru Blu Gum. Do you think celebrities
make products like foods or clothing cooler?
Do you think celebrities make good role mod-
els? If your favorite celebrity chewed Tru Blu
Gum, would you buy it and chew it, even if it
was bad for you or you didn't like the taste?

6. Maeve decides that Matt and Bailey are a
good match when she realizes how much they
have in common. How important is it to share
common interests with someone you care
about? Do you think a relationship can work
out even if the people in it are very different from each other?

7. What are some things can you do to help the
environment? How can you learn more about
environmental issues?

8. Maeve tells Matt that "girls like me and
science do not mix," and Anna and Joline
tell the BSG that the Sally Ride Science
Festival is for dweebs only. How do you feel
about those statements? What do you like or
dislike about science?

9. Even though Katani is annoyed with Reggie, she still helps him by telling him about the errors in his calculations. What would you have done and why?

10. Maeve idolizes Audrey Hepburn, and Charlotte admires Sally Ride. Whom do you look up to and why?

Charlotte Ramsey

Charlotte's Word Nerd Dictionary

BSG Words

Wicked (p. 14) adjective—*awesome; really cool*
Ri-donc-ulous: (p. 19) adjective—*ridiculous, outlandish*
Yummiliciousness (p. 133) noun—*tastiness that is even yummier than delicious*
Yuuugly (p. 144) adjective—*beyond ugly*
Dream-crush (p. 158) noun—*a guy who is like someone you might want as a boyfriend someday*
Glam-tastic (p. 162) adjective—*glamorous to the max*

Other Cool Words . . .

Luxuriate (p. 12) verb—*to indulge in luxury*
Chided (p. 50) verb—*scolded*

Bohemian: (p. 54) noun—*creative person who lives and acts without regard for conventional rules*

Subtle: (p. 60) adjective—*something that's almost hidden, that isn't obvious*

Spearheaded (p. 72) verb—*acted as the leader*

Handiwork (p. 85) noun—*a particular person's work*

Mischievously (p. 97) adverb—*teasingly*

Infamous (p. 105) adjective—*having a bad reputation*

Minions (p. 126) noun—*followers or sidekicks*

Atrocious (p. 154) adjective—*really bad; hideous*

Dubiously (p. 167) adverb—*doubtfully or hesitantly*

Sabotage (p. 168) verb—*to try to prevent someone from achieving a goal*

Notes from the Green Machine

Dear BSG fans:
We hope you enjoyed reading our latest book, *Green Algae and Bubble Gum Wars*. If learning more about the environment is your cup of green tea, we hope you will check out the BSG Green Machine club at beaconstreetgirls.com. Going Green is the way to go!

BSG forever,

Avery,
Charlotte,
Maeve,
Katani,
Isabel

Five ways *you* can be part of the BSG Green Machine today!

1. Going shopping? Bring a tote bag from home and reduce paper and plastic waste.

2. Why not give fashion recycling a try? You can find trendy treasures in second hand stores. It takes energy to manufacture clothes—re-wearing saves resources.

3. Walk or bike to your next destination. You'll save energy, reduce pollution, and get fit, too.

4. Reduce your average shower time from ten minutes to five minutes and you could save more than four thousand gallons of water a year! Wow!

5. Make a commitment to learn how you can help protect the environment!

Hey Girls:

Rise to the top of the Green class! Visit sallyridescience.com to checkout two book series, Our Changing Climate and Earth's Precious Resources. Each series has four books about our planet's changes, and what we can do.

Reminder from Charlotte:

If you are visiting the Boston area, don't forget to stop by my favorite museum—the Museum of Science in Boston, Massachusetts: www.mos.org

---

We think these resources are really cool, too.

epa.gov/kids/ : The U.S. Environmental Protection Agency's fun kids club includes games, pictures and lots of great info about the environment.

epa.gov/climatechange/kids/index.html : Fun animation about climate change rocks this site!

nrdc.org/reference/kids.asp : Meet the Green Squad and more at the Natural Resources Defense Council's website.

Share the Next

BEACON STREET GIRLS

Crush Alert

Love is in the air at Abigail Adams Junior High—there's a big dance coming up, and the BSG are having fun thinking up dream dates. But as the day of the dance approaches, things start to get complicated. Why is Dillon paying more attention to Avery than Maeve? And why is Nick spending so much time with Chelsea, when everyone knows he and Charlotte are made for each other? Who will the BSG share the last dance with?

Check out the Beacon Street Girls at

beaconstreetgirls.com

Aladdin M!X

Here's a sneak preview of the next

BEACON STREET GIRLS

Special Adventure,
Isabel's Texas Two-Step

A trip to her aunt and uncle's San Antonio ranch for Elena Maria's *quinceañera* should be a great adventure for Isabel. But Elena's brought four friends along, and is developing a serious diva attitude. Isabel's feeling a bit left out. . . .

The sun had set by the time we landed in San Antonio. People were laughing and joking as they left the plane. Even Aunt Lourdes looked more relaxed. *Must be the Texas air,* I thought. I smiled as I checked that I had put everything back in my bag. I hoped Elena Maria was in a better mood too, and would let me use her cell phone now.

But Elena and her friends were still totally wrapped up in their own world at baggage claim. Jill complained about how hot the airport was. Lauren was disappointed that she didn't see any cowboys around. Scott and Andrew put on their sunglasses and acted like they were a pair of cool dudes from the big city. I noticed that a lot of people— regular people—were walking around in cowboy boots. I really wanted a pair . . . ones with bluebirds on them.

"What's that music piped in overhead?" Scott asked.

"It sounds like we should all be holding hands and skipping in a circle or something."

"It's not that at all," Elena Maria answered sharply. "It's Mexican ranch-style music."

"That's a polka! My Polish cousins dance to it all the time," Jill said, laughing.

"No way that's Polish," Scott said. "They're singing in Spanish."

"Well, whatever it is, I like it," Andrew said. He grabbed Jill by the hands and twirled her. "Get used to it, Jill. I hear there's a lot of dancing at kinzy kinzy whatevers."

"Keen-seh-ah-niera!" I piped up.

"And I'm having a band," Elena Maria explained in a haughty voice. "At least there better be one, that plays a lot of hip-hop and soul and funk."

Ugh. One more second of *quinceañera* talk would make me cuckoo. And anyway, I really wanted to let the BSG know that I was in Texas! "Elena, can I please use your cell phone now to text my friends?" I asked.

"Okay."

I was about to take the phone, but all of a sudden we heard a loud whoop. It was my cousin Anthony, the oldest of my Uncle Hector and Aunt Inez's three boys.

"If it ain't the Bostonians! Welcome to Texas, y'all!" His voice boomed throughout the terminal.

"Tony! It's been so long!" Elena ran up to him. The two hugged like they were old friends. This was news to me, but then, she had been to Texas more times than I had.

He was tall. Dark. And from the goo-goo eyes Jill and Lauren were making at him, I could tell they thought he was way handsome. This wasn't the Anthony I remembered. Back then, he was goofy-looking.

When he saw my mother and aunt, he cut through Elena Maria's friends, leaving Jill and Lauren with stars in their eyes and Scott and Andrew looking a little intimidated by this handsome Texas cowboy.

"Tía Lourdes! Tía Esperanza! You ladies look hot!" He gave them big bear hugs. Tony was taller than everybody. His energy seemed to put more color in my mother's cheeks. Then he turned to me.

"Is this *la chiquita*? My little *prima* Isabel? Give your cousin Tony a big *abrazo*, little girl!" And before I knew it, he scooped me up. Whoa! Nobody had actually picked me up in years! These Texas boys were enthusiastic. I grinned from ear to ear.

After all the introductions, Tony said his mom had a big dinner waiting for us at the ranch. Since my stomach was growling, that was welcome news to me. I wondered how we were all going to fit in one vehicle, but when we got outside he pointed to a big, shiny, black Suburban SUV, the kind with three rows of seats and little TVs hanging from the ceiling. All the girls hurried to get a seat. "You're not going to believe the inside," Jill shouted to the boys, who were struggling to get all the luggage into the back of the car or lashed onto the roof.

"My mother is so excited about your *quinceañera*, Elena," Tony explained after we got on the road. "She and Dad are thrilled you're letting them do this for you. You know, my mother, she's always wanted a girl of her own. Guess me and Fonzie and Rico weren't cute enough." He laughed.

Elena Maria was silent. There was something about his words "letting them do this for you" that made her clam up. The awkward silence was broken by Lauren.

"Fonzie? Rico? Who're they?"

"Didn't Elena Maria tell you? Those are nicknames for my younger brothers, Alfonso and Ricardo. Don't tell them I told you, though."

Jill and Lauren exchanged sly looks. "We won't." They giggled in unison. I got the feeling that my cousins might be in for some girl trouble.

Sandwiched between Scott and Andrew in the far back row, I couldn't really see out the windows, but the scenery must have been interesting because both boys had their faces pressed against the glass. Meanwhile, Tony continued to act like our tour guide.

"We're heading due west of San Antonio. I think you Boston folks will find *Rancho Los Mitotes* very comfortable, with everything you need. Mama's set it up so that the guys'll stay with us in the north wing, and the girls and the two *tías* in the south."

Jill and Lauren grinned and looked at each other. I knew exactly what they were thinking. "Wings" equaled mansion! Mansion equaled swimming pools and princess-style bedrooms. I had to admit, I was excited too.

"Tell my friends more about your place, Tony," Elena Maria said, practically glowing.

"Oh, Elly-belle. That can wait. Believe me, you're all going to hear a lot more about our place than you'll ever want to know."

"Come on! Tell them. They're going to go absolutely nuts." She turned to her friends. "You are going to *love* this place."

Tony laughed, cleared his throat, and told a story he'd obviously told many times.

"We moved there when Rico was still tiny, about five years old. You know, big ears, missing teeth. He was a yuuugly little thing."

Boys, I thought.

My mom asked Tony to go on with his story. Tony beeped his horn at a big Cadillac emblazoned with a long-horn steer hood ornament and then continued. "We used to have a tiny ranch, just about a hundred acres further south from here, until we discovered a small pocket of natural gas on the property. My dad immediately sold it when we found this place. It's called *Rancho Los Mitotes*. *Mitotes* is a Spanish word for dances. Wait, maybe it's an Indian word. Anyway, it was used to describe the parties that the local people had a long time ago. They'd have feasts and drink and dance and do all sorts of festive things. Supposedly, our land was such a place where the Coahuiltecan people would gather."

"Kwo-weel-whaaat?" Andy piped up.

"It's pronounced 'kwo-weel-tek-ahn.' They were peaceful, and they sometimes lived side by side with the Spanish at the missions. We've never found artifacts or anything that proves they were there, but we know this ranch was established in the late 1800s. It already had its name by the time we came along, so there might be something to the rumor that it was a special place for the Coahuiltecans.

"Our ranch is unique in that, at the north end, the

terrain is Hill Country, with a bunch of live oaks and small hills, and to the south, it's mostly flat land—scrub, cactus, mesquite, stuff like that."

Scott leaned over and high-fived Andrew. I guessed they both thought they would be riding the range like old-time cowboys or something. The thought of all these city slickers dressed in chaps and hats appealed to my ridiculous side. I saw a cartoon in the making.

"Antonio," my mother said in Spanish, "tell them about the cattle operation."

"Sure, Tía. We've had a small cattle ranching business for about six years now. We specialize in Brahmans, and when you see them, you might find them a little strange-looking. But the beef is tasty and our cattle are known as the best around. We also have some Charolais, Red Angus, Herefords, and oh, I almost forgot—Elly-belle, you're going to like this—we've got a few longhorn steers now. They're really cool."

"Oh, no. I don't like that at all!" Elena Maria protested. "The last time I was there, I almost got chased down by a big, mean cow! I don't like cows with horns."

"Well, then you're really going to like our newest additions, the mini Hereford."

"Can you ride them?" Lauren asked.

I smacked my forehead. "Even I know you can't ride a cow!" Elena Maria put her finger up to her mouth. That was her signal to tell me not to embarrass her friends. I was beginning to think that I might not get anything right with my sister this week.

Tony thought about this. "Well, I guess you can,

but they won't go very far. They just sorta stand around and . . . chew cud." Tony looked at my mother. "Tía Esperanza, my father is going to ask you if you'd like to serve barbecue at the fiesta. He's famous for his barbecue."

Lauren and Jill let out a collective gasp. "We love barbecue!"

"Yum," Elena Maria exclaimed. "Sounds great, Tony!"

"Tony," I yelled from the backseat. "Is that natural swimming hole, the cavern or whatever it's called, still there?"

"The *tinaja*? Yes, it is, but if you want to go swimming, we've now got something better—a great, big, new swimming pool!"

My mother gasped. "*Ay*, Antonio. I'll bet that was your mother's idea."

"You got that right, Tía. Mom has wanted one for so long that Dad had one installed last Mother's Day. She never liked the *tinaja*. But I liked it. In the swimming hole, the water's always cool and most of the time, clean.

"Isabel," he yelled to the backseat. "We've had a lot of rain this spring, but the waterfall isn't running yet."

I clearly remembered the *tinaja*. It had this cool limestone outcropping that formed a half dome over the pool. When I was little it looked to me like the kind of place where fairies and talking animals would have tea parties.

The city was far behind us, and the night sky was filled with stars. Soon everybody grew quiet. The twinkling sky stretched before us.

Andrew broke the silence. "Wow. I can't believe how many stars are out tonight."

"Dude," Tony said proudly, "you're deep in the heart of Texas!"

Collect all the BSG books today!

#1 Worst Enemies/Best Friends   ☐ **READ IT!**
Yikes! As if being the new girl isn't bad enough . . . Charlotte just made the
biggest cafeteria blunder in the history of Abigail Adams Junior High.

#2 Bad News/Good News   ☐ **READ IT!**
Charlotte can't believe it. Her father wants to move away again, and
the timing couldn't be worse for the Beacon Street Girls.

#3 Letters from the Heart   ☐ **READ IT!**
Life seems perfect for Maeve and Avery . . . until they find out that in
seventh grade, the world can turn upside down just like that.

#4 Out of Bounds   ☐ **READ IT!**
Can the Beacon Street Girls bring the house down at Abigail Adams
Junior High's Talent Show? Or will the Queens of Mean steal the show?

#5 Promises, Promises   ☐ **READ IT!**
Tensions rise when two BSG find themselves in a tight race for seventh-
grade president at Abigail Adams Junior High.

#6 Lake Rescue   ☐ **READ IT!**
The seventh grade outdoor trip promises lots o fun for the BSG—but will
the adventure prove too much for one sensitive classmate?

#7 Freaked Out   ☐ **READ IT!**
The party of the year is just around the corner. What happens when the
party invitations are given out . . . but not to everyone?

#8 Lucky Charm   ☐ **READ IT!**
Marty is missing! The BSG's frantic search for their beloved pup leads
them to a very famous person and the game of a lifetime.

#9 Fashion Frenzy   ☐ **READ IT!**
Katani and Maeve are off to the Big Apple for a supercool teen fashion
show. Will tempers fray in close quarters?

#10 Just Kidding ☐ **READ IT!**
The BSG are looking forward to Spirit Week at Abigail Adams Junior High, until some mean—and untrue—gossip about Isabel dampens everyone's spirits.

#11 Ghost Town ☐ **READ IT!**
The BSG's fun-filled week at a Montana dude ranch includes skiing, snowboarding, cowboys, and celebrity twins—plus a ghost town full of secrets.

#12 Time's Up ☐ **READ IT!**
Katani knows she can win the business contest. But with school and friends and family taking up all her time, has she gotten in over her head?

#13 Green Algae and Bubble Gum Wars ☐ **READ IT!**
Inspired by the Sally Ride Science Fair, the BSG go green, but getting stuck slimed by some gooey supergum proves to be a major annoyance!

Also . . . Our Special Adventure Series:

Charlotte in Paris ☐ **READ IT!**
Something mysterious happens when Charlotte returns to Paris to search for her long-lost cat and to visit her best Parisian friend, Sophie.

Maeve on the Red Carpet ☐ **READ IT!**
A cool film camp at the Movie House is a chance for Maeve to become a star, but newfound fame has a downside for the perky redhead.

Freestyle with Avery ☐ **READ IT!**
Avery Madden can't wait to go to Telluride, Colorado, to visit her dad! But there's one surprise that Avery's definitely not expecting.

Katani's Jamaican Holiday ☐ **READ IT!**
A lost necklace and a plot to sabotage her family's business threaten to turn Katani's dream beach vacation in Jamaica into stormy weather.

Isabel's Texas Two-Step ☐ **READ IT!**
A disastrous accident with a valuable work of art and a sister with a diva attitude give Isabel a bad case of the ups and downs on a special family trip.

Have you seen

www.BeaconStreetGirls.com ?

Visit **BSG** Now!